FAE UNDONE

A CLAN FAE NOVELLA FROM THE ENCHANTED ROCK IMMORTALS

SUSAN PERSON

Copyright © 2020 by Susan Person

Cover Art by Book Cover Insanity at bookcoverinsanity.com.

All rights reserved.

No part of this book may be reproduced in any form or by any electronic or mechanical means, including information storage and retrieval systems, without written permission from the author, except for the use of brief quotations in a book review.

ISBN 978-1-953412-01-0

To all those afraid to take the leap towards your dream. You Can!

THE ENCHANTED ROCK IMMORTALS

Demons and Vampires. Elves and Fairies. Mages and Witches. Werewolves and Dragons. Psychics and Telekinetics.

These magical beings and more exist, rubbing shoulders in their daily lives with unsuspecting humans. But it doesn't happen without order. Millenia ago, the clans—Sanguis, Fae, Magic, Shifter, and Human Paranormal—wisely formed a Council to maintain that order. The end? To ensure the worlds of human and paranormal beings didn't collide and break out into a war that would result in the extermination or subjugation of either.

As human civilization progressed, the first council formed the All Clan Charter at the natural vortex in Great Zimbabwe, giving each clan a voice in the administration of affairs both between the clans and with humans. Next, Asia formed their council at Chengtu Vortex. Then the European at Warel Chakra Vortex. North America came next at the natural vortex humans called Enchanted Rock, in what today is known as Texas.

Now, thriving communities of paranormal beings exist in and around the granite outcropping. Humans scrabble over the dome, not suspecting an entire city exists within its confines: The North

American Council and all its departments—Legislative, Administrative, Security, Medical, Vortex Transportation, and Legal, plus restaurants, clan hotels, and shops catering to the paranormal crowds.

Also under that dome? Intrigue, politics, and most importantly, love. These are the stories of The Enchanted Rock Immortals.

FAE UNDONE

CHAPTER 1

Zander fell to his knees in front of me. His elven blond hair, cut short to blend in with the human world, stood out against his tanned, human skin. He, like me, belonged half to one people and half to another. His half was a more common occurrence, from when an elf seduced a human. If the offspring had powers, they were brought to our world to be raised as elf. The elves and fairies had their own alliance sealed when my parents married, and the product of it was me. *Half of each. The insurance to make sure both interests were represented from that point onward.* Unfortunately, both species banned it before and after the one instance. My problem too.

"Where are the coins?" Zander's fingers sifted through the sandy dirt. Small clouds of dust spun up in his haste.

Kalypso's army surrounded us. The uniformed crunches against the grit stopped as they took their places. My desperation increased. Life as her prisoner wouldn't be life at all.

"I found two." I coaxed them up from the sand. They drifted effortlessly to my palm. Relief settled over me.

"Here are some." He dropped them in my hand.

All small, but they would do. I pulled my hand to the opposite shoulder and tossed them into the air like feed for the livestock. *This I can do.* My palm cradled to my lips, I blew a small gust of air to suspend the coins. The slow descent to the ground would buy us a little more time.

The soldiers stood still like the statues at the gates.

Bright gold glinted in front of us. Five large coins with spokes. The Gods granted passage. I closed my eyes and held the coins over my head. *Thank you.*

I recognized the unison footsteps behind us from the training sessions held in the courtyard. They belonged to Kalypso's personal guard, the toughest and most loyal to her, and known for their brutality. To be captured by them meant torture or death... and those who were tortured wished for death.

I turned to face them. Kalypso's long, dark hair blew in the wind. Evil radiated off of her and embalmed my realm with misery. The wickedness twisted across the land and left the kingdom diseased. The North American Council didn't see her nefarious ways.

The NAC, the paranormal governing Council based in Enchanted Rock, Texas, consisted of a bunch of idiots unable to see closing the vortex wouldn't stop Kalypso from finding a way to their precious Enchanted Rock. The Fae traversed in ways older than the time the other clans had existed. Enchanted Rock existed because my ancestors created the vortex.

"We can spare one," Zander said.

"Not a spare. A gift." I flung the coin like a discus into the center of her guards. My lips formed an opening to send the wind to suspend the heavy coin. *Wind. Thank you.* "Let's get to the fountain."

The best of her mercenaries remained in place. All of them frozen for a day, at least, from that one. The time gifted us a head start.

We leapt to the first tiled steppe around the fountain. A cloud motif decorated each tile.

"Athena." Kalypso's voice boomed.

My chest tightened. My name on her lips chilled me.

Zander's hand slipped in mine and gripped like an anchor. "Ignore her. We need to get to the leyline before she gets to us."

We jumped hand-in-hand to the second tile set of tiles, painted to represent the pinkish hues of an early sunrise sky. The colors a perfect mirror of the sunrise on the beach, which was one of my mother's favorite places. My father commissioned the fountain as a tribute to my mother, while they were both alive.

"Come on. This is the straightest ride home." Cymone perched on the edge of the pool, where the tiles matched the lush colors of the vegetation. She tucked her wavy hair behind her ears and waved me forward. "We need to hurry." Her brown eyes met mine. She learned how to traverse at an early age. The process came so natural to her.

Straton stood guard to her left in position for us to pass through. His lean muscular frame towered over Cymone. *Always on guard.* His loyalty to me, and my father before me, were important, but his loyalty to Cymone endeared him as a friend.

A small smirk formed on Cymone's face.

"Did you get it?"

Cymone patted the bag on her hip. "Your diversion worked perfectly. We slipped in and out of your mother's old sitting room unnoticed."

I bit my lip. Celebrations would have to wait until we got back home.

"Athena," Kalypso repeated, my name poison on her lips.

My feet landed heavy on the tile next to Cymone. Zander's hand no longer held mine. I twisted to see him near Kalypso. *Too close.* "Zander, we go together." I jumped back to stand by his side.

"You three go ahead. I'll be right behind you. I'm going to make sure she doesn't follow." His lips touched my temple.

My chest tightened. It'd be an argument later. I held up a gold coin and slipped it into his back pocket. He battled some of the toughest opponents in the name of the kingdom but none like Kalypso. *Gods protect him.*

He leapt up to the next level to face her. His strong will would get him killed without me.

I took a step forward but lurched to a stop. Every muscle in my body tensed. I could join him. Straton and Cymone could travel back with the artifact.

Straton's fingers wrapped around my forearm.

I met his eyes. "Do you want to lose those fingers or shall we go for the whole hand this time?" It would grow back, but it would hurt like hell.

"Princess, we need to get you out of here. Capture by Kalypso would be death or worse, " Straton said.

My back to Zander, I stumbled into a jump and landed the level where Cymone waited.

"We only have a short window," Cymone said.

No one was better than him at combat. *Except me.* I looked over my shoulder at Zander. "Damn it." My stomach knotted. Our plan to retake the kingdom couldn't risk both of us. I hated to admit they were all right. *I'm not about to admit it now.*

"Athena." Cymone touched my arm.

She moved her hand back and forth. The water rippled, and our reflections disappeared. I took one last glance at Zander. Tears threatened. *Gods, I beg you. Don't let him die.*

I tossed the three remaining coins into the swirling water.

"Jump," she whispered.

We slipped through the liquid and traversed.

My mouth opened, desperate for air, as my head popped out of the water. I crawled out of the pool. Every time I passed from one to the other, I gasped like I'd been deprived of something vital for minutes instead of seconds. *Embarrassing. Three hundred and fifteen years old and I traverse like a fifty-year-old.*

Cymone pushed my hair out of my face. "This blonde mane of yours looks like a tornado whipped through it. I don't know why the path didn't remain stable for you, but I will do better next time."

We both knew her skill wasn't the problem. My best friend was an expert at calling perfect leylines to travel. Out of breath, I scooted around on the floor of the protected safehouse to watch the water. *One one thousand, two one thousand, three one thousand, four one thousand, five one thousand.*

Zander didn't come through.

"Where is he, Cymone?" I grabbed her hand. Kalypso's torture known to be worse than death. I'd rather be the object of her abuse than Zander. Panic riddled my thoughts.

"Don't, Athena." She wrenched my hand away. "It drains both of us. He'll be in his own time. It is his way."

"I need to go back. Kalypso would rather take me captive," I waved my hand in the motion to call my path. *Zander could still raise an army against her without me. I don't think I could without him.*

"No, you will abide by his wishes. Zander respects your requests, and you must do the same for him."

My heart pounded against the wall of my chest. Sweat beaded on my palms. "I can't not help him."

"Patience should be a lesson at the top of your list." She reached for the communication tool made of enchanted wire and twisted in ovals. One hung on each port entrance to communicate through the leylines. It didn't always work. If parties traversed together and got separated, it worked most times. "Zander," she whispered in the center.

"I missed my ride, but I'll find my way home." His thoughts

came through the apparatus so much like his own voice. Almost like he stood beside me.

I inhaled a deep breath and focused on the device.

Cymone held it towards my mouth. "I love you, Zander. Get your ass back here," I said into the center of the silver mess.

"I love you more, buttercup. See you soon."

Warmth circled my heart and spread out. *He's okay. Gods, please keep him that way.*

Cymone returned the contraption to its hook. "He'll probably have a headache."

"What? I didn't yell," I said.

"Your voice comes across much louder in the recipient's head. That's why I've told you to whisper." She shook her head. "Can I return you to the castle now?"

"It's not really a castle," I said. *But it was.* It was the smallest and one belonging to my family, and the only one Kalypso hadn't taken. We called it a cottage. My parents took me there when they wanted a break from royal life. Most of the other court members refused to go there, but the cottage brought back fond memories for me. Protections cast over it hid the identity of any who dwelled there.

"It is your home, Princess, and you are the heir to the kingdom." Straton placed a gentle hand on my shoulder.

"Thanks for the reminder. I'd rather wait here."

"Zander will be a while," Cymone said.

I narrowed my eyes on her. "Do you know something?"

"Only that he will not be home today, so you should tend to your duties. As their future queen, our visitors will want an appearance from you." She wrapped a towel around me from the constant stack kept by the pools. "Not as a drowned rat."

"They can wait. I'm not as eager to align our interests as they are," I said. "At least not until I know Zander is safe." The

Timberlands affiliated with Kalypso several times, but their greed prevented them from long lasting alliances.

"If you don't secure them as an ally, Kalypso will make sure they join her forces," Straton said. "And you are half fairy."

"She wants to use me to control the people because they don't trust her like they do me. She only rules by fear."

"If you don't make peace with the ones from Timberland, her forces will outnumber ours." Straton said.

I nodded. "You're right, but numbers aren't always what matters." Since my father died, the battle for allies among the four fairy communities consumed our lives.

"I don't trust them," I said. "The Timberlands."

"No one does," Cymone said. "But Kalypso already has the Leafspirals, and their numbers are great."

"Yes, I'm aware, and we have the Sandsifters. I'm not sure the Timberlands will turn on Kalypso, even if I offer them land and the seat on The North American Council. They consider her one of their own, and only the Gods know if that's true."

"The overture will have to be greater than anything Kalypso can extend to them," Straton said.

"That's what scares the Hades out of me." Rumors circulated across the kingdom the reclusive clan wanted a marriage within the royal succession lines. Only after my father's death did we learn they thought they'd succeeded when Kalypso married him. But she didn't produce a child. *Thank the heavens he never knew.* He thought he married a Leafspiral and would have never married a Timberland, with their tendency to deal in dark magick.

"I feel strange." I rubbed my head. Everything slowed down. Few could summon me like this. A pull stronger than any I'd previously experienced yanked me through a vortex. I hit the ground hard. I scanned for threats and found myself sprawled in the middle of the floor of the North American Council chamber at Enchanted Rock. I gasped for air. *Assholes. This better not be over some trivial shit, which why they usually summoned me.* No one else stood in the cavernous room. A tug in my gut led me to the Fae ward. Dread danced down my spine. *This can't be good.*

A Fae guardsman and a mage stood, as cold as the rock around us, on one side of Kalypso with her second in command, Zack, on the other. Power rolled off the mage. My gut burned with the fear of what master manipulation she dealt to force this audience.

"Princess Athena, I'm here to inform you of a joint decision between the North American Council and myself to maintain peace between the realms." Her voice filled the space around us.

I bit down on my tongue to keep my silence.

Kalypso smirked. "An exchange has been made for your life. You are hereby banished from Lanorinia and will remain on Earth. Any attempt to return will result in you being stripped of all your titles, as well as those of anyone who helps you. Anyone assisting you will be imprisoned. You will retain your seat on The North American Council at Enchanted Rock and represent the Fae as my proxy."

"I'm the rightful heir." I didn't give a shit about my titles, but I did care about my people, my friends, and Zander. Kalypso had terrorized the people in the short time she reigned, and the terror reached further every day she sat on the throne.

"If you had married Zack, we wouldn't even be here right now."

I snorted. That marriage wouldn't have changed anything. It was about control. "I want to speak to the Council."

"You can, of course, but it would be a shame for your friends to pay for that action. Besides, the Council has made it clear. This is a Fae matter, and they will support the peaceful decision." Her smirk grew across her face. "Zander is at my castle now under the care of my favorite guard. If you fight me on this, I'll let the guard do what he does best."

My heart raced at the finality of the decision. *I lost. My kingdom. My friends. My love.* I tamped down the urge to fight. The safety of those I love and the people of Lanorinia was more important.

A force yanked me from the room and spit me out on my feet in front of Enchanted Rock. *Has to be a rule against kicking a council member out of there like that.*

"Fuck you," I yelled and held both middle fingers high in the air at the giant domed rock.

CHAPTER 2

5 *Years Later*

THE ROCK WALL around the restaurant patio stood waist high. All of the restaurants on the mountaintop had some kind of outlook of the view. Jules asked me to come up here many times, but I'd avoided nature since my banishment from Lanorinia. The sight must be gorgeous when the skies were blue with white puffy clouds. That wasn't its current face though. Thick heavy clouds swirled and staked their claims. Thunder rumbled and shook. I loved storms. The connection to the elements in a raw form excited me.

The patrons didn't seem to notice. My group didn't seem to notice.

"You folks do see the wicked storm forming out there, right?" I took my seat at the table.

Jules, my closest human friend, sat opposite me. Had Zander and I not found each other, I might have ended up with her. Her green eyes carried light, and I occasionally got lost in them. The need to protect her lived in me like it did for Zander. She made life in banishment bearable, even happy at times, as happy as I could be.

She glanced over her shoulder. Her massive ponytail of auburn hair bounced. "Happens all the time. They never come this far. The jet stream or something guides them off that direction." She pointed along the ridge. "It's like a one in a million chance it will ever hit here."

This storm was no ordinary disturbance. I recognized the green, blue, and black disaster as it brewed in front of us. A storm meant to wreck, destroy, and kill anyone in the way. My heart sped up. This was the work of Fae. *A very strong Fae.* Only two Fae were capable of doing this.

And that storm wasn't mine.

I rubbed at the stiffness in my neck. "This is the one-in-a-million time. We need to take cover."

A funnel shape started to form in the sky. Darkness enveloped the horizon. Light-sensing bulbs lit the space on the patio. Sparks shot out from the contact of lightning on the mountain. My heart raced faster.

I jumped out of my seat. "Now! Where can we take cover?"

Jules' wide eyes met mine. "There's a wine cellar embedded in the mountain."

"Go there and take as many people with you as you can." I pointed inside. The tornado grew in diameter and inched closer. *Shit. People are going to die.*

"What about you?"

"I'm going to gather the people from here and meet you there," I said.

When everyone was safely off the patio, I opened up to the power and called my friend, Wind. *It's been a while, but I need you.* The dark force pushed back against my magick and Wind. I gasped at the strength. My hands trembled.

Not able to redirect it, I had to get the oblivious people inside, the ones that hadn't taken cover in the cellar, to safety. I didn't have time to tap each of them on the shoulder and ask nicely. The Council punishment would be swift if a Fae fight occurred in human sight.

Seek shelter. I sent the message out as far and wide as my power reached.

A zombie look covered the faces around me.

I hate this. Taking away their freewill. Even if for their own good. No matter how much I consoled myself, I'd always thought I was an ass the few times I'd been forced to take these measures.

The zombies turned and headed to the safety of the lower floor.

Through the glass, I could see them filing downstairs in a calm fashion.

Alone on the patio, my teeth gritted tight. "One last try." My hand up to the sky, the funnel came closer. I strained against the dark magick. *Too many lives to give up.*

The only thing left to do was try to put a protective bubble around the buildings. I'd never gone that far before. *I had to try.* I ran for the stairs.

People hunkered down on the steps to the wine cellar, packed in tight. I let go of the mind control to prepare for the bubble.

A few blinks and a slight haze of disorientation fogged the aura of the wine cellar. Awareness returned. Fear grew in the tight space. The Council's punishment be damned if these people saw my magick.

Jules waved me towards the group down at the bottom. I waved back with a weak smile. No way to get down there, and my invisible bubble would do more good here. The sight of my friend renewed my strength and confidence.

I turned my back to the stairs and dropped down in a crouched position. *These people will live today. Jules will live today.*

My hands spread wide against the floor. *Protection.* I envisioned the bubble and watched it grow. First around me. Then it encircled the people nearby and outward, until the entire building was engulfed with my magick. I called all the elements to me. *Wind. Earth. Fire. Water.* My strength pushed past the bounds of the restaurant and breached the walls of the buildings on either side. I sucked in a breath. *Protection. Harder than I thought. Push.* My head pounded, but the wall increased. My white light, invisible to the humans, engulfed the populated areas.

The funnel threw debris, mainly trees and rocks, against the shell. Each one created a tiny divot in my defense. The closer the tornado got, the bigger the fragments. Wind whipped against my wall. I dug my nails into the floor. Dug deep. Focused. Fortified the perimeter. My scalp tingled. Hair lifted. The wind blared like a steam engine. All other sounds muffled and deafened. Black walnut and hickory scented the air.

I am stronger than him. My confidence chipped but not broken from our last encounter, I drove the light defense against his destruction.

My ears rang in the complete silence. I opened my eyes. The storm dissipated, but everyone was frozen in time around me. "Fuck." I dropped the protection.

A large gold coin drifted across the air towards me. It hovered right in front of my face. I could command it, but the act would provoke him. He would take the insult out on these innocent people in a torturous fashion like his mentor, Kalypso.

"Athena, there you are."

My eyes cut to the right. "Zack." I inclined my head towards Zander's twin brother. Identical in physical appearances but not in loyalty or heart. Hatred festered under my skin and I readied my magick for a fight.

"Time for you to come home." He smelled like home. The salty scent of the coast drifted in the air. *Lanorinia. Zander.* My chest ached. The loss of my home and love never left me.

"You risked all these lives to extend an invitation for me to return to *my* home." Anger brewed in my gut. It swirled fast and sparks sputtered from my fingertips.

"Easy now. I had to do something to remind you. You've been away so long I wasn't sure you remembered what it was like to be Fae." He grabbed me and smashed his mouth on mine.

A sour taste formed in my mouth. I gripped his shoulders and shoved him back at arm's length.

I kneed him in the crotch.

He stumbled backwards, his posture rigid.

My jaw clenched. "I never forgot." *I never forgot how you supported Kalypso and betrayed my family and your brother.*

"Zander sends his love." Zack smirked.

The edge of my vision darkened. *Bastard. I could kill you with any of the elements.*

"I'm banished, and Zander is dead." The darkness wrapped around my heart. My hair extended out. Lightning ripped from my fingers into Zack's chest. I'd have to face the Council if I killed him here, but I could hurt him. *How can he live with himself?*

He captured my lightning and wound it into a ball. Unable to absorb it like me, his fingers opened, and he released it to the sky. Thunder rumbled overhead. He shook his head.

"Athena, come home for our wedding. You can't avoid our marriage forever."

Marrying Zack appealed to me as much as the vomit in danger of coming up.

"I've been gone for years. Why have you sought me out now?" I glanced at the coin. It sank to inches above the ground. The humans would unfreeze if the piece touched the floor.

"It's time to take your throne and me as your king."

I coughed through a guffaw. "No way is Kalypso going to let me have the throne, and I love your brother. Dead or alive. How can you even think you could come close to filling his place?"

"I have a signed contract promising marriage, and I want my throne." Zack approached it like a business transaction, whereas Zander's heart led his decisions. He regarded everyone's life above his own, which was how Kalypso captured him that day at the palace.

"Well, wish in one hand and..." The coin glinted a half an inch from the floor. I held out my hand and called the piece to me. It spun on the narrow edge in my palm. I flung the gold coin towards Zack.

His head shook from side to side in disapproval. The coin landed at his feet. Strong but not as prepared for me as he thought.

I smiled, smug in my own actions.

The gold expanded into a small puddle under him, and he dropped through to the leyline path. His voice echoed out. "Zander is alive." The traverse would be miserable, since I called it. *At least I hoped so.*

His words bounced around my head in the same echo. My mind allowed my heart a little somersault at the idea. *Could it be true?* I pushed his statement aside as another lie from Zack. *If Zander was alive, he would have come to me by now.*

With the coin gone, the people resumed their actions. I stepped out of their way, my movement seamless, as if time hadn't just stopped. Patrons and staff emerged from the cellar one by one. Some moved towards the windows and others to the patio. I walked out on the patio and breathed in the after-storm air to cleanse myself of Zack.

Fingers wrapped around my shoulder. I turned with my arm up on instinct to break the hold.

"Whoa." Jules held her hands up. "The storm really freaked you out, huh?"

"Something like that," I mumbled under my breath.

She hugged me. "It's okay."

I wrapped my arms around her. "I'm glad you're okay." The Council forbade the Clans from telling humans about magick. I had to keep it my world to myself.

We joined the others on edge of the patio to take in the expected devastation. Of course, the damage all occurred outside the boundary I'd set.

"It's like we were in a bubble," Jules said.

"Yes, looks that way." I chuckled. "I guess we were lucky." I wished I could tell her the truth, but the lies I told protected her.

"Someone was watching out for us today," she said.

"I need a drink."

"Shots?" Jules raised an eyebrow.

"Absolutely." I smiled. Not the smug smile I gave Zack, but a genuine one for my dear friend.

"Good. They have your favorite here." She grabbed my hand and led me to the bar. "Two of your Turquoise Rum Shots." She held up two fingers to the bartender.

"Make them doubles?" he asked.

"Not yet. We have to make sure you know how to mix first."

The tall, way-too-perfect-looking bartender flashed her a smile as white as the ones on a toothpaste commercial. "Oh, I can mix."

I turned my head and rolled my eyes.

Each distinct scent drifted toward me. Coconut. Pineapple. The bite of alcohol. My mouth watered in anticipation of the sweet burn. It would take a lot more booze than this to give a Fae a buzz, but I wanted anything to help erase the memory of Zack and his lips on mine.

Too-perfect bartender placed the drinks on the counter. Four of them, instead of two.

I reached into my pocket for cash. "How much?"

"This round is on the house." He caught Jules' gaze. "To prove my mixing skills. I'm Tom, by the way." He leaned his elbow on the counter, bringing himself closer to her.

"Thanks for the shots, Tom." Jules winked and headed towards our table with the free drinks in hand. She could charm any man. I'd think she was Fae, if I didn't know better.

"I'm pretty sure he thought he was going to get your name and number." I took a seat in one of the tall chairs.

"He might still. He's pretty hot."

"But he knows it. Such a turn off," I said.

"It wouldn't hurt for you to do a little flirting…and maybe some other stuff." She held out a shot glass for me. "Cheers."

Our glasses clanked. Not the high-pitched clink of crystal, but a low, thick glass *clank*.

I downed the bluish-green liquid. The slight burn slid down my throat to my belly. I relished the heat. The only thing strong enough to erase Zack's assault or Zander's love for a brief moment. My eyes burned. The torment in my heart attested to my 'no flirting' rule.

"Let's do the other one." Jules handed me the second round.

We downed them.

"And we're going to get you some D tonight." Jules' eyes were already glassed over from the booze. "It's my mission tonight."

The pain in my chest fluttered. "I think you mean you are going to get some." I winked at her. *I couldn't do that to Zander.* Although it didn't happen for all Fae, the lucky ones found their true mate and bonded for life. Lucky, that is, as long as you weren't bound in a marriage contract to another.

"He must have really done a number on you," Jules said. "Or you have an awesome vibrator. If it's the latter, I need to know where to buy one." Her smile wore the drunken version of its normal self. She pushed my shoulder.

I giggled. "I'm good." Fae mates didn't focus on gender like humans. It wasn't unusual for Fae without true mates to have multiple partners in their relationships, but Zander would forever be the only one for me. I held my breath against the heartache.

"How about another round?"

"I'll go get them." She kissed my cheek and pulled the ponytail holder out, tossing her long auburn hair over her shoulder.

That guy has no idea. She's in full on prowl mode.

I watched her maneuver up to her target. Part of me envied her freedom. The other part of me only wanted to be in Zander's arms again. Zack's false hope, "Zander is alive," haunted me. My heart folded in on itself.

CHAPTER 3

I covered my head with the pillow. *Gods. Again.* It did little to drown out the rhythmic bang of the headboard in the other bedroom.

Sleep avoided me most nights. The distress Fae, especially elves, experienced when separated from their true love never subsided. My focus during the day provided a space of control around it, but my subconscious freed it at night.

"Damn." I sucked in a breath and rolled out of the bed. The wood floor, cold against my feet, turned to the even chillier tile in the bathroom. *Maybe the shower will help drown them out.*

Water sprayed out of the shower head. I ran my fingers under it waiting for the right temperature. It hit my forehead and ran down. Zander's image stuck in my head, just like every other day. *Damn Zack for lying. Damn Kalypso.*

Coolness pressed against my neck, even though hot water ran over me. I opened my eyes.

A whisper of a voice trailed against my ear. "Athena..."

I spun to look around for the source. My feet slipped on the shower floor. Fingers pressed against the smooth tile wall for balance. Five years. Five heartbreaking years since I'd heard his voice. The soft warm sound absent for far too long. Not even in a whisper. My heart fluttered in my chest.

"Zander..." I murmured back. It's not like there was anyone else to hear. *Zander can't be alive. Kalypso killed him.*

"Zander! How?" Tears spilled down my already wet cheeks. *Is it really his voice coming through?*

"Hi, love." His voice, soft, soothed away the years of loss in a moment.

My heart pounded so hard I put my hand to my chest to hold it in. "Where are you? Can I come to you?"

"No," he said, his voice a shout.

I grabbed my head with the other hand. "Now, I understand the need to whisper. Why?"

He chuckled. "It's not safe here. I'll find a way to you."

"Are you alive? Where? When?" Some Fae communicated from the next life but not often.

"Soon. I lo..." His voice stopped in mid-sentence. "No, Zack." His shout pierced.

I crumpled to the shower floor. "Zander?" I whispered. "Zander?" *Another game from Zack to torture us both? Or just me?*

My legs folded under me. I sat on the floor and waited. My fingers became water logged and pruned from the moisture. *Zander is alive.* Tears fell with abandon. *Always a cost.* Elf and fairy tears contained tiny pieces of our life force only the elements could replace. The price, unknown at the time, would reveal itself later. *What would it be this time? Would saving Zander, only to let him go, be the cost?* The thought cemented me to the floor for a long moment.

"Damn." I pulled myself up out of the shower. "I have to go back." *The second I step on the soil of my birthright, I will be bound to marry Zack.* But I couldn't let him torture Zander anymore. At least I assumed that's what I heard. Either way, Zander lived, and the drive to save him blotted out any fear for myself. *I can do this. I will do this. I'll see Zander, if only to say a real goodbye.*

I METICULOUSLY FOLDED EACH GARMENT, even the damn jeans, into the duffle. The attire in Lanorinia differed from what humans wore, especially in America, but I packed some of my favorites. The act only delayed the inevitable step of traversing to my kingdom.

The desperation to see Zander grew every second. To lay eyes on him again. My heart flitted like a lovesick teenager's. To not touch him. A hell my arrogance brought upon us both by believing Kalypso's message she'd killed him.

My butt sank into the bed. Father wanted the people protected. I'd failed once. Success wasn't optional this time, and the odds were against me. Kalypso and Zack at the palace versus me with my rusty magick.

I couldn't ask Zander to fight his brother, and he wouldn't want me after I killed Zack.

A soft knock rapped on my door, and it opened.

"Hey," Jules said.

"Did you already get rid of Mr. Too-Perfect?" I asked, my voice light. I tried to sound normal.

"Yes." She smiled and leaned her shoulder against the door jam. "And his name is Tom." She scooted the bag and sat down beside me. "Are you taking a trip?"

"I'm going home." A limited truth settled better than a blatant lie.

"Hmm." She studied me. "Why does it sound like you're not coming back?"

"I'm not sure when I will be able to." I clasped my hands together and stared at them. Tears burned in my eyes. *Don't cry.*

You don't know what the tears will cost. I took a deep breath and faced Jules.

Her eyes reddened with dampness in the corners. She turned and sat cross legged and reached for my hand. "So, don't go."

"I have some family business I need to take care of, and my stay could be a permanent commitment."

"You don't sound very happy about heading home." She grabbed my hand. "We all have choices, Athena, which means you don't have to go. Or I can go with you, if that will help. I have a ton of unused vacation time."

I squeezed her hand. "No, my home is no place for you. I wouldn't put this burden on a friend. Especially not one who means as much to me as you do." My gut told me Jules could handle the Fae realm, but the Fae wouldn't know how to handle her. The Council took swift action on those who broke the rules. Jules belonged here.

"It's not a burden when you are doing it for your best friend." She squeezed my hand tight.

"If I didn't think you'd be in danger, I might take you with me." The words came out before I thought them through.

"Wait. You're in danger? No way are you going without me then. I didn't take self-defense classes and learn to shoot a gun for nothing. I learned those skills to protect the people I care about most."

She meant what she said. After five years of friendship, I knew Jules' sincere voice.

"A different kind of danger." If only self-defense techniques and guns worked against Kalypso, I'd already have evicted her from my father's throne.

She narrowed her eyes on me. "What other kind of danger is there?"

"Family drama."

"Trust me. I know family drama. I'm coming." She hopped off the bed. "I'll go pack a suitcase."

I forced a smile. "I'm leaving in thirty minutes. Can you pack that fast?" I made up my mind to leave while she filled her suitcase.

"Of course, I can." She paused in the door way. "I'm excited to see where you're from, since you never talk about home." Then she disappeared.

I slid my hand in the pocket of my jeans and pulled out the coin I kept for emergencies. The metal burned in my hand, like the lie burned in my chest. I guaranteed disappointment for all those who loved me. *I suck.*

My hasty steps, muffled by the tennis shoes I'd chosen, helped me make my way out to the pool. With the coin in my palm, I looked back one last time at the house.

I'd left my kingdom in the hands of a murderer and an opportunist, and I had to face my fate.

"Sorry, Jules," I said over my shoulder.

My hands moved back and forth, and the pool water swirled on command. I tossed the coin in as an expert traverser would. As any Lightliner would. No matter how perfect I called the leyline, the ride would be rough. Another sign of my failure as the child of a gifted Lightliner who traversed with ease.

I took a step back and prepared to jump. Three steps into the run, a rustling noise came from behind me. Too late to stop. One coin. One chance. I leaped.

Arms caught me in mid-air. Jules and I fell through together. One coin. *Damn it. I have to hold on to her. I couldn't let her land in a random spot in Lanorinia.*

I gasped for air as soon as my head cleared the pool. "Jules?" I didn't see her. *Maybe she came out first.*

Someone's hand latched onto mine and pulled me free of the water.

I looked up into the warm brown eyes of a friend. "Cymone." I smiled. She looked the same as she had five years ago. Not that we aged much in a half a decade.

Cymone's lips made a tight thin line. "Princess Athena," she said, her words formal.

"I'm not forgiven then," I said. She asked to join me in the human realm, and I'd refused the request. "Where's Jules?"

Cymone's brows came together. "Who?"

Auburn, wavy hair floated up in the water. My legs weakened and made the steps toward her labored. "Jules." I pulled her out and laid her flat on the floor. Her skin paled. My fingers pressed to her throat and found no pulse. I checked her air passage. "She's not breathing."

Cymone knelt by my side. "You brought a human here?"

"Help me." I thrust my hands against Jules' chest. *Gods help me.*

Jules coughed. Water ran from her mouth.

Thank you. I sent a silent prayer for Wind to carry and flipped Jules onto her side. More water poured out.

"You're okay?" Her eyes still appeared a little unfocused.

"Yes." I covered my mouth with my fingers to stifle a sob. "But you? You shouldn't have followed me."

"You can't swim," Jules said. "Where the hell are we, Athena?" She pushed herself up to a seated position.

"Jules, we need to send you back." I glanced at Cymone. The Fae tolerance for traversing was much higher than a human's. "How long do we need to wait before we can safely send her back?"

"Hold up. You're not sending me anywhere." She looked up at Cymone. "Hi. I'm Jules by the way." She held out her hand.

Cymone regarded it with a raised brow but shook the offered hand, "Cymone."

"Nice to meet you," Jules said. "Now, someone tell me how we fell through a swimming pool and landed here. And where is here?"

The Council rules for the human realm stated memories should be wiped, but we were in my kingdom. Lanorinia's Court had similar rules, depending on if the Seelie or Unseelie handed down the judgment. Jules deserved better than a lie or memory wipe. *The truth it is.*

Cymone narrowed her eyes at me. "If you tell her, you only bring more danger on her."

A shadow fell across me. "Princess?" Straton had the worst timing.

I squeezed my eyes shut. The majority of the air in my lungs forced out and braced for Jules reaction.

"Princess?" Jules declined my hand to help her stand. "Someone better start explaining." She crossed her arms and looked at me.

Straton took a knee in front of me. "Welcome home, Your Royal Highness, Princess Athena Alexandria of Lanorinia. Our rightful Queen."

His esteem and loyalty meant so much. The formality, however, ate at me, and I already owed Jules an explanation. He earned my respect a long time ago.

I extended my hand to his. "I'm not Queen yet. Stand up before you freak out our guest even more."

Jules' mouth gaped open. "And you never thought to mention this? And where the fuck is Lanorinia?"

"Your Highness, they will already know you're here. It will only be a matter of time before they find you," Straton said.

"Yes, Straton. I understand the consequences of my return. Father wouldn't have approved of hiding."

"He would, if only until we found a way to resolve the contract."

Gut punch. "Trust me. I haven't forgotten. I'm fully aware of what I must do. Maybe we should take a seat and have a drink," I said. "A quick one."

"Shall we?" Cymone gestured to the small dining room at the safehouse and led the way.

"Fine, but I am severely pissed at you." Jules crossed her arms and glared as she followed Cymone.

Cymone poured drinks for all of us. She took the chair next to me. Jules sat in the seat across the table. Straton stood like the soldier he'd proven himself to be.

"What do I even call you?" Jules eyes narrowed on me again.

Straton cleared his throat. "You must address her as Her Highness, or as Princess Athena or —"

I cut my eyes at him.. "She can call me Athena, like she has for the last five years. You know how I hate the long formal titles." I didn't miss the look Straton and Cymone exchanged. Their unspoken questions required answers, but I wasn't ready to give them. Not until Jules was safe. I looked at Jules. "Athena. It is my name."

"Don't play games." Jules slammed a hand down on the table.

Straton took a step forward.

I held up my hand. He stopped.

Jules' eyes opened wide. "So, these people just follow your orders."

"These people are my friends," I said. "Like you."

"Am I? They seem to know the truth."

"They've known me a little longer is all," I said. "But I thought about telling you several times."

"And they know you're a princess or a queen or whatever."

"She is the rightful queen by birth but has yet to be crowned. She's officially the crown princess until then," Straton said.

I rolled my eyes at him. "Thanks, Straton." I focused on Jules. "You are in my kingdom, by birthright at least. Lanorinia."

"My brain is on overload." Jules grabbed her forehead. "And how did we get to Lanorinia?"

"You traversed through the leylines between our worlds," Cymone said.

"Our worlds? We're not on Earth?"

"Yes," I said. "And no. We are in a part of Earth humans would never find on their own."

"And we did that through water?"

"Water makes for an easier travel experience for most. Not all require it." Cymone cut her eyes at me. "Some are gifted. They will be granted passage on a leyline path without direct water contact. It can be a rather rough ride when called by someone else." Her lips twitched, like she fought a smile.

She must have heard how I sent Zack back. I'm surprised he told anyone.

"Why were you on Earth?" Jules rubbed her temples. "Or the human part of Earth?"

"Because I was forced into a marriage contract, but my departure left my home and my people in the hands of a murderer." Regret daggered my heart for leaving.

"You ran away?" Jules' forehead wrinkled.

"She was banished," Straton said. "Based on non-compliance with the contract under the guise it would bring peace."

"We counseled her to stay with the humans until we could find a way to void the contract," Cymone said.

Jules ignored him. "And you came back why?"

"To take back my kingdom and accept my fate of a marriage to a man who I do not love."

"Sounds like just about every other royal marriage out there," Jules said.

I inclined my head towards her. She had a point.

Cymone kept her voice low. "Except she is not like every other royal as you know them. She controls the balance of magick in our world."

"And you can't tell anyone about Lanorinia," I said.

Her hand covered her stomach, and she let out a big belly laugh. "Who the hell would believe me if I did? They would send me straight to the state hospital." While good fodder for conspiracy theorists, she had no idea how much danger revealing my world to hers would put her in from the North American Council.

"I will send you back as soon as it is safe," Cymone said.

"Uh... no. I'm not going anywhere until my best friend is out of this marriage contract thing."

"We don't have time to argue over the impossible. They already know I'm here." I dropped my head and paused. My eyes met Cymone's. "Zander is alive."

"I know."

I narrowed my eyes. Betrayal burned in my chest. "You knew and didn't tell me?"

"You refused to take me with you," she snarked at me. "We've made several unsuccessful attempts to rescue him. Kalypso has heavy protections on his cell." She let out a breath. "And we knew you would come to Lanorinia to rescue him. Your kingdom needs you to liberate them, not join the people as victims."

"You are my best friend. You should have told me. I'm going to rescue him like I would have if I'd known he was alive years ago."

Straton broke my thoughts. "I will escort you, not only as my duty, but as your friend."

"You're not leaving me behind." Jules stood up and moved beside Straton.

Cymone followed. "Then the matter's settled. Your team accompanies you to the castle."

They formed a line, more like a brick wall, in front of me.

Jules glanced at Cymone. "There's a castle?"

CHAPTER 4

We traversed to the same pool we used the day of my banishment. *Gods don't let that be an omen.* We approached the heavy metal gates Kalypso installed after my father died. The sight unsettled me. A hard pit formed in my stomach. The monstrosity created a hideous divider among our people, a separation Father never would have allowed. *They would come down, by the Gods.*

Only a handful of guards stood on duty. No need for more. The magick on the gates only allowed them to open for certain people. The guards moved to either side of the path. Zack approached from the shadows, his presence solidifying what I long suspected. He and Kalypso monitored the leylines for activity. The safehouses weren't really safe anymore.

"I'm delighted to see you, Athena."

I straightened my back. "You may address me as Her Royal Highness Princess Athena Alexandria of Lanorinia." I wielded my titles like a sword to jab him. They meant nothing, but I resented Zack's familiarity with me.

"As your future husband and king, I think I can call you Athena." He plastered a smug smile across his face.

"Or not. You will address me with the proper respect of my rank until we are married."

From the other side of the gate, he bowed. "Yes, your Royal Highness."

"That's the marriage contract dude?" Jules whispered.

"That's him."

"He's kind of hot. Too bad he's a douche bag."

"Yeah. And I'm in love with his twin brother."

"Ouch," Jules said. "The twin brother is the bad breakup?"

I nodded. "Zander. Only we never broke up."

Zack laid his hand on some type of pad near the gate. White light peeked out from underneath. The gates groaned and opened to allow our passage. He snapped his fingers and left our sight. No doubt to alert Kalypso of our arrival.

The hard pit in my stomach grew by ten as we crossed the threshold to the castle. Palm trees lined the pathway. Manicured space surrounded the trees. Statues alternated with massive geodes, a tradition carried over from my father. I'd chosen many of the rocks from the base of Mount Hades for very specific reasons. Love from my parents radiated here, memories of when they taught me to care for the geodes and plants.

My childhood home, this special place, was infested with a diseased rodent.

I turned my hands in a slight motion. Fingertips extended out to accept small charges as I passed the crystal. Not enough time to draw large amounts of power, but the bursts would be like an energy drink for humans.

The walkway opened up to a large fountain in the courtyard. The trek not nearly long enough for my taste. A gag formed when the bronze front door came into sight. I'd be a prisoner in my own home and bound to someone I didn't love. But my friends would be safe and leave with Zander, and he would be free after years of captivity.

The guards uniformed march, several steps behind us, halted at the bottom of the stairs.

My eyes followed the familiar site of the enormous doors to our family insignia at the top. On the other side of the door, footsteps thundered on the marble. I recognized the sound. Kalypso and her guard.

A little surprise wouldn't hurt. Should I? Yes.

I formed a triangle with my thumbs and forefingers. A bright light formed within my own personal power plant. My eyes closed, and I envisioned the path for the energy. The intensity reached the appropriate level. I let it fly against the doors. "Sorry, Dad. I know you loved those." *Not sure if he can hear me from the next phase of life.*

The force sent the doors skidding across the floor in a metal against stone shriek. They slid to the feet of Zack and Kalypso. Both stood with eyes wide open as soldiers flanked them.

A smile born of pure satisfaction spread across my face.

"Did you plan to make such an entrance?" Jules smirked.

"No, it came to me along the walk."

"I like it," She patted my arm.

"Athena, welcome home." Zack bowed. "As always, all eyes are on you."

"As always, you're an asshole."

"Athena." Kalypso stood tall, dark hair pulled to the back. No curtsey. Her claim on the royal seat staked. She did sit on it after all. The image of her on my father's throne filled me with disgust.

"Kalypso." I offered no curtsey to the fairy either.

Cymone curtsied and Straton bowed, both stiff in their actions. They only performed the requirements of self-preservation.

"Come. Let's talk the terms of your marriage," Kalypso said, straight to business.

I shoved down my desperation to get out of the contract.

"I'll talk terms once Zander is free." I stood steady on the outside of the doorframe. To enter without my claim would be agreeing to her terms without negotiation.

"I'm sorry. I didn't realize you thought there were options, Athena. We can ask the rest of your friends to wait in one of the cells, if that helps." Kalypso's fake smile plastered across her face.

Jules positioned herself between us. "Do you know who you are speaking to?"

"A human?" Kalypso looked past Jules to me. "You brought a human to our world." She laughed a deep, dark cackle. "Is she a sacrifice?"

"Sacrifice?" Jules' wide eyes looked at me over her shoulder.

"Humans never leave our world," Kalypso said.

"The Council does not allow us to kidnap or sacrifice humans." *Anymore.* I wrapped my hand around Jules' arm and pushed her out of the middle of us.

Straton took my queue and maneuvered her behind him.

Kalypso looked at Zack. "Bring the prisoner to the main chamber. We'll meet you there."

"Yes, my queen."

The urge to give Zack a magick shove quelched by the realization Zander was the prisoner.

"Come." She motioned with a crooked finger pointed in the direction of the room.

Zander. In moments he would be in front of me. Tears filled my eyes. I fought them back. Kalypso would not see me cry today. I would not pay the cost of Fae tears in front of her, especially with my friends and Zander at stake. That price was too high.

Jules slipped her hand in mine. "Everything's going to be okay. We'll get this bitch."

My voice wouldn't work. I forced a smile. A shiver went through my body.

"You're not worried about her. You're nervous to see him."

I swallowed the hard lump in my throat. "Yes." So many times during the first couple of years, I'd fantasized about a reunion. Then I'd refused to let myself entertain the idea. My heart leapt forward and pounded in beats faster than our steps.

We made the corner to enter the room. I deflated. He wasn't there. Nobly dressed members of the Court representing both Seelie and the Unseelie stood on opposite sides of the room. Light versus dark, but all were her supporters. *Not surprising.*

Kalypso gestured towards a u-shaped configuration of desks and chairs. The Seelie, made up of the Sandsifters and Lightliners, and Unseelie, comprised of the Timberlands and Leafspirals, each took seats on their respective sides. Three chairs remained on the short middle piece of the U. The one in the center mirrored my father's throne.

Not mirrored. This was my father's throne. She'd changed the fabric to remove our family insignia, but I knew his throne. *The bitch will pay for everything.*

"Shall we?" Kalypso raised a brow.

To take a seat beside her and not the throne would mean I conceded to her terms and recognized her as queen. *No way in Hades.*

Zander entered the room, flanked by Zack and the guards.

My heart sprung to life and woke the rest of my body. Years of tension fell away to oblivion. My true love and I stood in the same room for the first time in five years. My sights narrowed on him alone.

My Zander focused on me, but imprisonment changed him. Dirt smeared his pale skin, his blonde hair longer than before, and a beard grew on his once clean-shaven face. The full lips I loved to touch were barely visible in the middle of the scruff, but they parted to show his best smile.

My heart flipped in my chest. I returned his smile. Everything in me wanted to run to him. *Stay put, Athena. Wait for the right time.* Awareness of the room's onlookers returned to me. The court members would see any move toward him as a betrayal of the marriage contract. Betrayal of the contract meant none of us walked out of here alive.

I knew it.

Zander knew it.

By the smug smirk on her face, Kalypso knew it.

My gut twisted when I met her gaze.

I turned my wrist and opened my hand to receive a magick boost. *There would be no greater satisfaction than blowing her out of the realm.* One good lightning bolt could take her head off and end this. Sparks bounced between my fingers.

Zander's head shook from side to side in the slightest gesture.

I cocked my head.

He mouthed one word, "No."

My mouth went dry. I didn't see any other options, but my trust in him outweighed my need to kill Kalypso. My fingers curled up in a tight fist, and the energy passed into my body, leaving tingles in the wake.

Kalypso moved to the throne as if she owned it. She gestured for Zack and me to take the seats on either side of her.

"I'll stand. Thanks." I crossed my arms. Zander clearly sent a signal to me not to kill her now, but I couldn't give up the kingdom so easy after spending five years in exile. I assessed the room for coins. *Gods, now would be a good time to send some.*

"As you wish, Athena," Kalypso said.

"What is the nature of this session?" The Unseelie leader asked.

"We're here to decide the fate of a traitor."

"I've never betrayed my kingdom." *How can she even suggest I'd be a traitor to my own?*

"Not you, Princess." Kalypso's eyes cut over to the side.

I followed the path. *Zander. Not happening.* Firm fingers wrapped around my forearm. I met Straton's eyes. He'd stopped me from going back for Zander five years ago. *No one would stop me today.*

He let go.

Kalypso babbled on about Gods know what lies. I edged over to Cymone and whispered. "Get them out of here. You're the only one who can." I took a step away. "Do it now."

Cymone nodded and maneuvered between Straton and Jules. With a hand on each of their shoulders, they were gone.

I had no illusions I'd be granted passage. Kalypso expected me to do something, but she had no idea how strong my Lightliner magick had grown, even without much practice. I closed my eyes and let a slow breath out. No coin needed to freeze everyone in the room. The only problem, Zander was frozen too.

The freeze wouldn't last long without a coin, but I only had the one in my pocket I took from the safehouse. I stood in front of Zander. My lifeforce depleted fast without a coin to freeze this many people, and my body shook from the strain. I needed to wake Zander to traverse. Electricity crackled at my fingertips. The jolt had to be small enough not to affect the others, but big enough to wake him. I placed my hand over his heart, the rhythm slow and steady, despite his lack of movement. *Just one little zap.*

Zander sucked in some air. "You should've left."

"We're both going to the safehouse. Then to my cottage, where the protections should still be in place. I'll apologize now for the ride." My hand gripped his shoulder. I dropped the coin between us and waited for the water to spread under our feet, so we could gain our freedom.

"Wha..." Pain exploded through my back. My head butted against Zander's chest. His arms wrapped around me, and we descended into the puddle. The throbbing spread up my spine. My field of vision narrowed. We bobbed up out of the water, and everything went black.

CHAPTER 5

Voices shouted through the fog around me.

"I told you I didn't mean to stab her."

"I should kill you, brother." The last word sounded bitter, like a witch's potion.

Light peeked under my eyelids. Pain spiderwebbed across my head. "Zander?" Rough and weak, my voice didn't sound like my own. I cleared my throat and tried again. "Zander?"

A hand slipped in mine. I rubbed my thumb across the scar behind his pointer finger. "Zander."

"It's me, love. I'm right beside you."

I opened one eye first, and then the other, the room's light harsh against my sensitive eyes. The medicinal scent hit me, distinct to a clinic space at the cottage. I pushed my free hand down against the bed for leverage. An intense ache radiated across my lower back.

Zander's other hand pressed against my shoulder. "Don't try yet. You need to heal first."

"Why is it taking so long?"

"Zack planted a short blade in your back."

The memory rushed back to me. I fell against Zander when I called the leyline.

"I didn't mean to, Athena." Zack came into focus. He knelt beside me.

Zander let go of my hand. He wound the collar of Zack's shirt up and lifted him. "Get away from her." Zander shoved his brother back hard.

Straton drug Zack out of the room.

"Where are Cymone and Jules?"

Zander kissed my forehead. "They went to gather some herbs. Cymone knows a potion to help you heal faster."

"How bad is it?"

Zander's eyes squinted tight. When he opened them, they were filled with tears.

I reached up and touched his cheek. Love mixed with relief warmed me. "Hey. I'm here. I'm okay. Tell me what needs to heal."

He kissed the palm of my hand and took a deep breath.

"The knife pierced your spinal cord at the base." His eyes searched mine.

I let out a breath. My back twinged in response.

"It's not like it's life threatening, Zander. We regenerate. We heal. Well, unless someone removes our heads or blasts us with dragon fire, but there haven't been dragons in a millennium at least." My attempt to make him laugh failed, and my body ached. I noticed the numbness for the first time. I tested my extremities. My legs were useless. *That's unusual.*

"Yes, elves do. You're half fairy."

"But I'm half elf too. I've had injuries before. This pinky finger is my third." I wiggled it in front of him.

He shook his head. "I think the pain concoction Cymone gave you is getting to you."

"She gave me the good stuff, huh?" My words slurred. Even I noticed. "Why are you worried?"

"Cymone didn't like how slow you're healing. That's all." He pressed his lips to my forehead, and his whiskers brushed against my skin. His touch almost unbearable, and I wanted more.

"My eyes feel like they weigh a ton." I fought to keep them open, wanting to look at Zander's face after all this time. I didn't care about sleep, but my body had other ideas.

"Close them and rest, Athena. I'm not going anywhere."

LANORINIAN SPICED INCENSE mixed with lavender enveloped me. Cymone's not-so-secret mix of aromatherapy she used to relax tension in the body for healing. Whispers drifted to me from voices I recognized. *Zander and Jules. They're talking.* It warmed me to hear them getting along.

I pretended to be asleep. Kept my breathing even.

"She loves you, Zander. Only you."

"My heart is hers just as it has been for the last three hundred years."

"You move way too slow," Jules said.

I fought back a giggle. *She's right, but to be fair, we were preoccupied trying to make sure the peace was stable after the Elf-Fairy Alliance formed.*

"How do you know she loves me above all others?"

Zander. My heart hurt he even questioned my love still. He is, and always will be, my infinite love.

"She would scream your name out in the middle of the night. I thought it was just a bad breakup or maybe you had died. I'd slip into her room and hum the lullaby my mother used when I had nightmares," Jules said.

I winced inwardly. *She heard? Awake I could control it, but asleep there was no awareness. That explains the soft tune that would get stuck in my head.* Jules comforted me when I needed it most, and I wanted to hug her. She soothed my torment, and I didn't know how I would repay her.

"When an elf is separated from their one and earnest, it can be painful. We unknowingly give up a piece of our immortality in exchange for a piece of theirs. Our people believe the separation of our soul causes the suffering."

I'd never believed the pain was real until my own experience. My heart hurt and the ache spread through my body.

"Was your pain like hers? Did you scream?"

Zander's silence made me want to open my eyes.

His voice wavered. "They sedated me every night. My screams woke half the castle for months. Kalypso wanted me to suffer, but Zack thought the sedation was a mercy." Zander paused. "It wasn't. The torment didn't stop. Only my ability to react to it."

Maybe I didn't believe he felt the same way. Maybe I didn't want to let myself think it. To think of him afflicted would have broken me more than I already was.

"Did Zack know you still felt the pain?"

"No, I didn't tell him." Zander said. "I promised my father I'd protect him from the world. That includes me."

"Don't you want to kick the shit out of him for all this?"

"Yes, but I made a promise. Besides, he loves Athena too. I don't think he meant to hit her with the knife. He's skilled with control of the weather, but he's never been good at throwing knives."

"You belong together, Zander. You and Athena. Don't ever question her love for you again or I'll kick your ass."

"Thank you for loving her when she was alone. When I couldn't be there."

Yes, Jules, thank you. I had no idea. My thoughts drifted into sleep.

THE COMFORTABLE SCENT, lighter than before, hung in the air. Cymone must have put the incense out in sand. "Hello?" I sat up in the dark room. *No ache or twinge..* I hung my feet off the side of the bed and scooted forward. They sank into something hard but not the floor.

"Ow! What the..."

"Zander?" I drew my feet away from him.

"Yeah." His shadowed form stood up in front of me. "Do you need some help?" He flicked the light on next to the bed. The room brightened in a soft glow. His beard gone. The face I knew well and missed for five years stared back at me.

I swallowed hard. Heat trailed down to my belly. My stomach fluttered.

It made me nervous to be alone with him after all this time. "Where is everyone?" I asked, my thoughts fuzzy.

"Asleep in their rooms."

"Why were you on the floor?"

"I didn't want to leave you." He shoved his hands in his pockets.

Five years of separation left us in an awkward place, where it was easier to talk to others about how we feel than to share those thoughts with each other. Though I hadn't told him before, he was my one love. Both elves and fairies can love many people, but only one is a lifetime love. Any before or after could be called a distraction. If he didn't love me, my life would be miserable when he did find his. He suffered as I did when we were separated. He must feel the same.

"Any sign of Kalypso or her guard?"

"No. We brought you to your cottage. Cymone said the protections the mage cast on it are still up."

He remembered I called my home the cottage and not a palace or a castle.

"Cymone's friends are always welcome here. Were you able to get the mage back safely?"

"Yes, and she was grateful for the asylum while she cleared her name."

I nodded. "I understand the need of a safe place." I paused. "We can't hide here forever," I said. "I've violated my banishment, frozen the court, and escaped with a prisoner. Pretty easy for them to track us down, since there are only a few places left for us to hide. They might not be able to summon or locate us from here, but Kalypso knew what she was doing by leaving one castle for me. We need to hit them hard and fast."

"No. We need a solid plan before we confront her again." He lowered his eyes to the thin gown someone had dressed me in.

Heat rose in my cheeks. My body didn't look much different from the last time he'd touched me, but his gaze on me was. The intensity caused my heart to race in response. Not sure if I'd respond with fight or flight. Maybe a little bit of both.

His gaze roamed my body as he continued. "Cymone's mage friend cast a very strong protection around the castle, and Cymone added her own magick to it. We should have protection for a few days."

"We probably shouldn't wake everyone tonight then. They need to rest up." My breath quickened. Zander's woodsy smell drifted around me. The space between us too much. I wanted him closer.

He placed a hand on either side of me and lowered his face to mine. Every feature of his as I remembered. He pressed his lips to mine in the gentlest caress, as if he was afraid to break me.

I tried to deepen the kiss, but he resisted.

"How much better are you feeling?" he asked, his voice rough with desire. The awkwardness of a few minutes ago flitted away.

The heat from my cheeks traveled down my body to concentrate between my legs. I wrapped my arms around his back and pulled him to me. "One hundred and ten percent."

CHAPTER 6

My stomach rumbled. The delicious aroma of bacon drifted around us. "I'm starving," I said into Zander's neck. I inhaled his scent, the euphoric sensation from his fragrance a reprieve from the pain of the last five years. Last night was real. He laid on the bed with me, and I treasured the time. I pressed my head to his chest and let the rhythm of his heartbeat sync with mine.

"I can make you hungrier," he whispered against my forehead.

I tilted my face up to his. My cheeks glowed like hot coals. I never considered myself safe in the last five years, but in Zander's arms, security seemed real. My internal guard discarded in a pile of ash as I burned under his gaze.

His lips brushed mine. "But Cymone will knock on the door any second to check on you."

"Fine. Let's face this day." I sat up. The sheet dropped around my waist.

Zander eyed my breasts. "We can be quick." He leaned forward and wrapped his lips around my nipple. His tongue swirled.

My head fell back, and I wound my fingers through his hair. I missed this, missed Zander, missed us. I needed him in every way I could get him.

Tap. Tap. Tap. "Athena? Are you awake?" Cymone called from the other side of the door.

Ugh. No. Cymone deserved a response. She healed my physical injuries many times over the years. I studied Zander. He healed the rest of me. My heart. My soul.

"Fuck," Zander whispered between my breasts.

"Yes, we'll be out in a minute," I yelled.

"A minute? That's no fun." Zander wagged his brows.

"The price of leading a rebellion."

"Yes, love." His lips scorched a path up to my mouth. "The rebellion can wait."

A twinge of guilt kicked my side. "Actually, it has waited years while I wallowed in my own pity. You suffered because of me. I don't know if I'll ever forgive myself." I swiped at the hot tears in the corners of my eyes. *No tears allowed.*

"No," Zander said. "Don't. You were banished and did what you thought would save us all."

"I abandoned my people. I abandoned you." Guilt swelled and poured out in streams down my face. "I should have just married Zack. Then Kalypso wouldn't be in control."

"Fuck no." Zander's face reddened. "If you had done that, you would have been her prisoner too. You almost were this time." He entwined his fingers with mine. "And no one will call you his wife except me."

"You would have been free and could have led the rebellion."

"There was no scenario where she would have ever let me go free, and the kingdom needs you." Zander took my face in his hands and wiped away the tears.

Always a cost.

"She planned to use you as a pawn either way," Zander said.

"Yes, her plan was to use me against you, regardless of what you chose." The dam of guilt cracked. "You forgive me?"

"There is nothing to forgive. I love you, Athena. 'Til the day we die and even after."

The tightness in my chest loosened. I kissed him with gentle caresses.

"Time to get dressed and begin the prep work to take back your kingdom." He stood and pulled me to my feet.

For the first time, I felt fragile, like a flower with only one petal left to lose. My feet planted on the ground, but I swayed, my legs unstable.

Zander wrapped his arms around me. "I've got you. I will always support you."

"Let's do this." I smiled up at him. Hope built in me, and I planned to share that hope with the rest of my followers.

We dressed and made our way downstairs for breakfast. A spread of items filled the fourteen-seat table in the morning dining room. Bacon, toast, eggs, jams, biscuits and gravy, covered the table. The plates in front of my friends all sat empty.

"Why is no one eating?"

"We are waiting for the Queen," Cymone said.

Queen. The title changed everything. I had to save the kingdom.

"You never have to wait for me," I said. "Well, unless it is the last ferry of the day across the channel. Then waiting would be good."

Laughter filled the dining hall.

I sat at the place square in front of the bacon. Jules sat to my left, and Zander took the seat to my right. He pulled the plate of bacon to us and gestured for me to go first.

"You better get what you want, because I'm hungry enough to eat the entire platter." I swiped a piece and took a bite of the crispy bacon.

He smiled. "I'm glad you're so hungry." He winked.

"In the future, Your Majesty should sit at the head of the table," Straton said.

Buzz kill. "That might be tradition, and we might choose to observe those customs on formal occasions, but we will not force tradition or formality when it is just us. I want to be comfortable in the company of my friends."

"Yes, My Queen," Straton said.

"And when we are alone, no one is required to call me queen or your majesty. I am Athena to you today. Just as I was Athena yesterday or five years ago." I expected Straton to argue. "Informal situations need to have freedom to speak."

Almost like they planned it, forks full of food shoved into the mouths around the table. Except Straton, of course.

"Yes, Your..." he paused as if it were a struggle for him. "Yes, Athena."

I bit off another piece of bacon. "Now, let's start brainstorming the plan to get my kingdom back."

WE DISCUSSED FAILED ATTEMPTS. The team came up with a plan, but I came up with my own. My strategy sat near the front of my mind and wasn't for anyone else to know. I could take Kalypso out once and for all on my own.

In the past, the Lightliners used freeze magick on her and her troops after they cornered her. They failed, because they didn't know how to keep her imprisoned. If I called all the elements to me and fired all my magick at her, I could banish her or even kill her.

The downside for me, if I dumped my magick at Kalypso, would be the drain on my lifeforce. If it didn't replenish, a premature permanent death would be my fate. I hated the thought of leaving Zander, Cymone, Jules, and Straton, but the chance to end Kalypso's reign meant more than my life. They would stop me if I told them. *This plan stays with me.*

Zander stared at me, his gaze focused and intense. He unnerved me, like he could read my mind. His eyes shifted to the rest of the group.

He gestured across the sketches and plans the group worked through. "This strategy isn't going to work." His voice, the one which commanded my father's armies, demanded attention and respect. He didn't use that voice very often, but when he did, people listened.

The room grew quiet and waited.

"Athena, I know you don't believe these options. I see the truth on your face."

Shit. He fronted me out. Maybe he had learned to read minds while I was away. "No, they might." I lied. My plan, the one I kept to myself, stood a chance, but none of the others they put together would.

"But you are not convinced, and we cannot lead an attack when our Queen doesn't have confidence in our strategy," he said.

"It's not that I don't believe in it," I said. The lie burned in my chest. I couldn't tell them I had faith in something I didn't. "No, you're right. I don't think any of the plans will work."

"So, you've decided to sacrifice yourself to take her out?" Cymone pursed her lips and stared at me. "Which is why your eyes glazed over when we were planning."

I shrugged my shoulders, not at all surprised they drew the same conclusion. "We each have sacrifices to make. There is a reason all four elements respond to me, and there aren't many approaches to rival the punch the elements can deliver."

"But we can take her out together," Cymone said. "If you trust us, you don't have to sacrifice yourself."

Trust for them I had, but this was about fate. The elements chose me for a reason. The same reason my parents kept my affinities a secret, so I would be able to use them when the right time came.

"No way in hell are you sacrificing yourself," Jules said. "But can someone tell me what I am missing?"

"Athena is powerful. Her parents were both from old powerful magick families. The power in her is what Kalypso wants most," Cymone said. Her calm demeanor concerned me.

"So, you think you'll just kill yourself to stop her?" Jules narrowed her eyes on me. "That's stupid, Athena."

To a human, the idea sounded insane, but to Fae, we knew how fate worked and understood the price of tears. Many of my tears still went unpaid. This was the cost. The resolution settled with me on how entwined my fate was with Kalypso's defeat.

Zander grumbled, "That's what I implied."

Jules slapped his upper arm with the back of her hand. "Someone like Kalypso, that's a stupid name by the way, isn't going to stop if you kill yourself. She's a power-hungry bitch, and if one source is depleted, she's just going to move on to the next."

She made sense, but my plan included taking Kalypso with me.

Jules stepped closer to me and lowered her voice. "What if the next person she preys on isn't as strong as you? Or what if she goes after someone else you love?"

Her argument was valid. If Kalypso lived and I died, the burden would fall on my friends. The guilt panged deep in my heart. *I can't fail.*

"For a human, she is wise," Cymone said.

Jules zeroed in on Cymone with a laser-like stare. Cymone didn't flinch, but it made me squirm. I wasn't sure who would win in a fight between them, but I didn't want to see it come to a scuffle.

"She's not the average human." I placed my hand on Jules' shoulder and squeezed.

"Aren't I though? My life will be short. I have no magick. Isn't that how you all judge us?" She looked around the room, making eye contact with each person. Her eyes landed on me last.

"I see you as my friend first. Magick or years lived doesn't matter."

She laid her hand over mine and squeezed tight. "Then take my advice like a friend would."

I blinked back tears and nodded. "You have my word." I looked around. "And we're going to need a better plan." If we could come up with a stronger strategy, I'd gladly accept it over mine. I didn't want to die and leave them, but I tucked my alternative away, in case.

Cymone pointed a finger in my direction. "If you can change this one's mind, you might have some magick in you, Jules."

CHAPTER 7

I sat on the ground by the lake and connected with the earth. I chose a quiet spot near my castle. A small breeze tousled my hair. *Hello Wind.* Light rippled across the water. Peace.

The meditation centered me, and I stood to take in a long view of the moon's dance in the sky.

A hand slid around my waist, and Zander's hip bumped against mine.

I leaned into his side.

"If you break your word, Cymone will not forgive you." His voice lowered. "And neither will your new friend, Jules." He and Cymone shared a jealousy over me and my friendship with Jules. I wasn't sure if the concern stemmed from the time lost with them when she was there for me or because they feared I would leave them behind for a simpler life in the human world. *Living in the human world would be easy, but who would protect my people? I thought I protected them by not being in the realm, but I was wrong.*

Zander knew me better than the others. He figured out I hadn't abandoned my plan. I inhaled deeply and let it out to a slow count of five.

"If I don't break my promise, you will all die."

"Death is nothing to me, Athena. We all die, whether we live a hundred years or a thousand."

A lump formed in my throat. I pressed my head against his shoulder and rolled until my forehead rested on his chest.

Zander hooked his finger under my chin and lifted until my gaze met his. "If you die, nothing is left for me. I sat in a prison cell for years, kept alive by the hope I might touch you again." His hands cupped my face. "I won't live without you."

I pulled back, but he held my face firm. I saw a touch of anger in his eyes, but I saw more love. Love drove his actions. "I'm only one life."

"One very special life. One I refuse to live without."

Pangs of guilt shredded my insides. *Damn it. I don't want to leave you.* The self-condemnation made me mute.

"Don't do it, Athena. Stick with the plan we have. I looped Zack in. He's on our side now."

"I—"

Bright white light bore down on us. My feet lifted from the ground. I tried to wiggle free, but I couldn't move. *What in Hades?*

Zander's head still remained in the same position. He hadn't moved. *Frozen.*

I couldn't even open my mouth to scream. I was frozen too. My eyes the only body part I could move, so I cut them to the left and right in expectation of an attack from Zack or Kalypso.

The bright light faded into a swirling tunnel, and I slid through.

My ass struck soft ground with a hard thud. "Ow." My palms against a green meadow, I pushed up to stand and readied for a fight. Sparks bounced between my fingers.

The bright sunshine here contrasted sharply to the night sky I'd left. A forest encircled the meadow. Crisp, clean, snowcapped mountains could be seen over the deep green treetops. This wasn't Lanorinia or the human realm.

I sensed someone near and spun into fighting stance.

"Wh..." My parents stood in front of me. I slapped my hand over my heart. It pounded hard like it wanted out. I gasped for air. "What kind of trick is this?" I scanned the forest line for Kalypso.

"No trick, Athena," my father said. The outline of the trees was visible through his ethereal form.

"You're not really here." My shoulders dropped.

"We are here. As here as we can be." My mother stretched a hand out toward me.

My hand met air when I tried to touch her. Everything seemed to slow down. I wanted to hug her, but the ethereal version made it impossible. "I don't understand. Why haven't you spoken to me before?"

She floated closer to me, unable to make contact. "We're not allowed to appear in Lanorinia or anywhere among the living," she said.

"We had to bring you here, and even then, there can be consequences," Father said.

"I'll take them," I said. No consequence seemed too great to see them. "I've missed you so much."

"Don't be so quick to accept a responsibility which isn't yours," he said.

"And we have missed you too." My mother smiled. I'd forgotten how magical it was.

I beamed at the sight.

"We brought you here, because you are about to make a grave mistake."

Father's translucent fingers waved over my cheek, unable to touch me. He left his hand in place, as if he could stroke my cheek, and a slight vibration emanated. It was almost imperceptible, even for me. "It's not about trust, Athena. It is about the future of the Fae. Your death would be the undoing."

"I'm one person."

"One person who will prevent an entire dimension from being wiped out," he said. "One person who will lead in a way even the Council couldn't predict."

I snorted at his mention of the Council. "I don't see why I matter so much."

"You will in time, but we need you to trust us for now," Mother said. She smiled and moved her hand over my arm. Her caress caused a similar sensation to the vibration from my father. *Love. It was love.*

I closed my eyes against the tears and opened them as Mother's hand wrapped around mine. The vibrations increased.

"If you attack Kalypso alone, you will die, and you will take all of the Fae with you," Father said. "The entire Fae realm will be undone."

Truth echoed in my ears. He was most certainly being honest. Even in death, my parents protected me. Tears spilled down my cheeks, and I turned to wipe them away. *Did they carry a cost here? Wherever here is...*

"I will not attack alone." I turned back to empty air and a faint and distant whisper on the breeze carrying their voices. "We love you."

Only the green meadow and forest remained. My throat thickened, and I pushed back any more tears. Bright light washed over me and sucked me into the tunnel. I landed on my ass again, in front of Zander. My thoughts were too disoriented to explain the events to him. Not sure I ever could.

He unfroze. "Did you fall down?" He narrowed his eyes at me.

"Yes," I said. "I will not attack Kalypso without our team or our army."

He extended his hands and pulled me to my feet. "Do you mean it this time?"

"I do."

His lips pressed against mine with full force. Warmth began in my chest and radiated out to my extremities. Heat found its way into my belly and my most intimate areas. His hands slid into my hair and drew me closer. A moan escaped my throat. His hardness pressed against me. My knees buckled. His strength held me in place.

He drew a breath. "Let's go inside."

"Too many people." My own voice was a ragged whisper.

"The woods." It wasn't a question.

"Yes," I said.

He scooped me into his arms and carried me deep into the woods where no one would hear us. Our hands everywhere, clothes seemed to fall off in our haste. Tree bark scraped my back and intensified my urgency.

Light shimmered around us like diamonds. I should control my power, but the release felt too good. The flora and fauna grew around us as an extension of my pleasure and tickled my skin.

Zander put one hand under my butt and lifted me up. The other hand threaded through my hair and cradled my head. My legs wrapped around his waist. Our lips melded together. He pushed inside me and stroked slowly at first.

"Call to me." His voice was rough in my ear. He bit down on my lobe.

"Zander." My own voice, thick with passion. I returned the bite by sinking my teeth into the muscle between his neck and shoulder.

He stroked faster and faster. "Athena." His words, deep and low.

We hit the pinnacle together and slid to the forest floor.

Zander kissed my forehead and my cheek. "You are my one true and earnest love." His lips caressed mine.

"And you are my one true love." I looked into his eyes. "Always."

CHAPTER 8

Cymone and Jules grinned like mad women when we rejoined the group.

"All the plants started blooming around the castle," Cymone said. "We were about to investigate, when we heard some noises drift up from the lake."

"Have fun?" Jules asked.

I rolled my eyes and ignored them.

Zander gave my hand a light squeeze.

"We need a new plan," I said. "We're taking Kalypso down." I looked into the eyes of each of my friends. "Together."

"Where is Zack?" Zander asked.

Everyone exchanged baffled looks and shrugs.

I locked eyes with Zander.

"Damn it," he swore under his breath. "I knew he was lying when he told me he wanted to join us. Spying like always."

"He only knows the old plan, Zander," I said. My smile started small and expanded.

Zander nodded, a smile forming on his face. "Yes, and we can use that." He rolled one of the maps out across the table and used salt and pepper shakers as weights to hold it in place.

"The strategy session couldn't wait until after dinner?" Cymone laughed. "Our queen needs to replenish her strength."

Jules giggled.

"I think I liked it better when you two didn't like each other," I said. "We have to make a change in our plans."

"What if we hit them here." Zander pointed to the map. "Two days before they expect us. I know you didn't want to attack near a village."

"Especially not that one, but it's a solid advantage point." I looked at my personal guard, my friend. "Straton, will the troops be here in time for us to maneuver them into place to intercept Kalypso's army?".

He shook his head. "Not all of them will arrive in time." He paused. "But if we have them by pure surprise, we might have enough to make a significant impact."

"We need to inflict a massive blow," Zander said. "If we're going to take Athena's ancestral palace back."

IF ZACK BETRAYED us like we expected, the plan would work. As much as he and Zander resembled each other, their personalities and morals couldn't be more different. Our success, even our survival, likely depended on him being the untrustworthy bastard we all thought him to be. *Please don't choose this moment to have a conscience, Zack.*

I watched Zander doing what he did best. He strategized with the different levels in the military hierarchy. His skill and navigation impressed. *He will make an excellent king.* My own thought caught me off guard. He would be the king of this kingdom. *A half elf and half fairy queen and a half elf and half human king.* Like a blustery wind, what my parents had tried to tell me registered. Zander and I each were half, so even though the joining of cross-Fae was not permitted, any kids we would have would be part of both. *Would Zander even want kids, knowing he is half human?* Being half human in the Fae world was not easy. The Fae half didn't count for much, unless the Fae was exceptional, like Zander and Zack, and they were born to a high-ranking elf. The story Fae told was they were stolen from their mother by demons in the dark to pay a debt to the elf who was their father. *No wonder Zack is fucked up. I don't know how Zander managed to not be.*

CYMONE, Jules, Straton, and I sat perched at a distance above the ravine, and I wondered if our plans would be enough. If I had done enough. My parents told me dying wasn't an option, and I listened. I listened to their instructions. I listened to Zander when he told me to stay back. I didn't know the tradeoff would be him on the front lines. *One of us has to go, and it can't be you.* His words echoed through my head. My stomach cramped. If the future of our world depended on me, then it depended on him too. We both had to survive. My realization came too late. *He is out there now.* Our decision had to play the hand dealt. Trying to change tactics now would be more of a risk than Zack.

I peered over the edge and located Zander. He maneuvered the military factions into place as they arrived. Some of the elves in the nearby village had volunteered to help. They were loyal to me by default. We chose this area because of the great love they had for my parents. As soon as we arrived, we were met with the gratitude and honor for my parents' legacy. Doors opened and my heart warmed in reminiscence of the precious times. Some of my favorite memories of my parents lived here. I first laid eyes on Zander here. An easy smile spread across my face. He was a young dutiful soldier from a noble family. Few of the other soldiers wanted to befriend the half human, until my father acknowledged his skills. He'd bowed to my father, but when he rose, his eyes locked with mine. Butterflies flipped around my stomach at the memories.

As if he remembered too, Zander looked up from the bottom of the ravine. Even from this distance, I could see the gleam of his smile.

The mountain shook, and the world slowed down, if only to me. The elf half of me tried to maintain perfect balance, but the fairy side let me fall to the ground. Adrenaline surged through my body. The jolt of the hard impact stole my focus. I clapped my hands against my temples to stop the dizziness. Dust drifted up my nostrils, and my heart sank deep. My ears rang for only seconds, replaced by screams. Dread dominated me. *Attack. We were hit.* To my left, Straton helped Cymone to her feet. To my right, Jules coughed but looked unharmed. I pushed myself up, resting my hands on my knees.

Straton bent in front of me and studied my face. "My Queen, are you injured?"

"No, I'm fine. Check on Jules," I said, my attention on the cliff.

He nodded and moved towards her.

I inched up to the edge of the ravine. Fear gripped me. My Fae vision homed in on the destruction. Rubble remained where a once thriving crossroads village stood. Unmoving bodies laid twisted in morbidly strange positions. Others, partially buried in the debris, scattered among the ruins of the village. Those elves standing upright shocked, locked in the moment, still as statues. A deep sadness invaded my chest. Red glinted with hints of gold everywhere I turned. *Elf blood.* My gaze followed the fragmented trail to the area Zander occupied moments ago. I exhaled. At that distance, he should be safe from the explosion. The trail of devastation continued, though. The ground gaped open like it had been ripped apart. I searched the crowd for Zander's face. *Nothing.* My legs shook, and the weakness came on strong.

A hand pulled my arm around a set of shoulders, and an arm slid around me to hold me up. I twisted my neck to see Jules.

"Straton says we need to get you out of here."

The words registered at a painful pace. *No.* "No, I'm not leaving. I need to find Zander."

"Straton and Cymone have already gone after him. They told me to get you out of here, but they knew you wouldn't leave without Zander."

"Jules." I removed her hand from my shoulder and stepped away. "Stay here." I ran towards the cliff's edge at full speed.

"Athena!" Jules yelled behind me. "Stop!" The terror in her voice gave me goose bumps.

I'd apologize later.

I leapt from the edge and executed a perfect swan dive towards the tree canopy below. Jules' screams followed me down. My mind opened to the forest and found the path. I flipped to angle my rear towards the ground. The trees accepted my request and cradled my fall like a jumper landing in a net. They passed me from cradle to cradle in a guided line to the last place I saw Zander. My feet lowered to the ground with the grace of an elf. I glanced around at the wounded military members. I didn't see any serious trauma among them, but the village would be different. *There are villagers injured too. That's where Zander would have gone.*

In my haste, I hadn't thought it through. I was too low to the ground to get a line of sight to use the trees again. My gut said Zander was already there. Dread chilled me. I called for Wind to push me across the ground as I ran. It gave me extra speed.

I came to the edge of the village. The overwhelming weight of grief hung in the air. My chest became heavy. The scene was much worse than I thought. No structure remained standing on this side.

Everything that once stood was nothing more than rubble. Blood soaked rubble. The blood of villagers. *The blood of my people.*

My fists closed so tight nails dug into my flesh. Dismembered bodies. Dozens of them covered the remains of the village. People missing limbs stood or laid in pools of blood. *The wrath I bring down on her will rival the vengeance of the Furies.*

Extremities would grow back, a luxury of being elf, but only if they didn't bleed to death and only if they didn't lose their heads. I knelt down next to a woman missing a leg and a hand. These people, my people, needed help now, and Zander was tough. *He'll be fine. Knowing him, he was helping people too.* There wasn't much medicine in my pouch, but I asked the earth to send me healing powers. I rubbed the little bit of mixture between my hands until it turned into a crystal-like powder from the touch. *I'm not a gifted healer, but Gods help me heal this woman.* My palms, covered in the magick-infused mixture, pressed against the open wounds. *For the love of my people, heal them.* Power coursed through and out of me like a shock wave. When I opened my eyes, I expected to see destruction from another explosion. Instead, my people healed. The missing appendages grew back at unprecedented rates. Not without a cost though. Moans echoed as new hands, arms, legs, and feet appeared. Wounds closed at an abnormal pace. *Is this one of Kalypso's tricks? A part of her trap?* I sat back on my haunches. *Now what?*

"Athena?" My name drifted to my ears. "Was that you?"

I twisted around to see Zander standing a few feet away. He covered the space in a couple of big steps. His eyes looked me over as he patted me down.

"Are you okay?" He took my hands in his and inspected them.

"I'm fine," I whispered. "What happened? After the bomb, the second shock wave?" I struggled to get my thoughts out in a coherent way.

"I don't know. The first bomb came from the other direction."

He glanced back and then at me. "I followed the strength of the second one here."

"But it doesn't look like anything else happened. I don't see any new damage." I scanned the scene, trying to understand what happened.

He squeezed my hands tight. "But something did, Athena." He smiled with tears in his eyes. "You happened."

CHAPTER 9

We doubled up the military personnel in their tents to create vacant ones for the surviving villagers. The cook had been instructed to feed them until they were full. Most wouldn't eat much. They grieved, and I grieved with them. The uninjured military men would build several funeral pyres tonight and match body parts to bodies where possible. The task would surely take them through the night. I wanted to stay and help, but Zander insisted I rest. I didn't have any fight left in me when we walked through the opening of our tent. The tent, my father's from war time, was in pristine condition. The space included a large table with maps and chairs, and a bed in the corner. Zander had been quiet, for the most part, once we made sure all the villagers had shelter and food for the night.

"What the fuck, Athena?" Jules raised her hand towards me.

Straton threw his arm up, and her hand connected. "Striking a queen is punishable by death."

"Damn it." She waved her hand and narrowed her eyes. "I wasn't going to hit her, and she's not my queen."

"I did jump off a cliff in front of her, so I deserve it." I shrugged at Straton.

He shook his head in slow motion. Not sure if the head shake was meant for me or Jules.

"You did what?" Zander roared and marched towards me.

"The trees caught me." I flicked my wrist back and forth.

"You are only half fairy, and you don't have wings. You cannot fly," he ground out.

I'd never seen him so angry. He frightened me a little, but I could still see love in his eyes. "I didn't use my fairy half. I used my elf half."

"Can we come back to that later?" Cymone asked. "I need to know what happened in the village."

"A bomb went off." Jules crossed her arms.

"Yes, and afterwards? The second seismic disruption." Cymone didn't address Jules. She focused on me.

I squirmed under her scrutiny.

"That was Athena," Zander said through clenched teeth.

"We don't know it was me." I rolled out one of the maps on the table and looked at the area where I was when it happened. I glanced at him.

His shoulders relaxed a fraction. "The source of power led me right to you."

I grappled with the truth and wanted to deny it. No Fae possessed that kind of power. I reached for Zander's arm to steady myself. "That doesn't make sense. No one can heal like that. Not an elf. Not a fairy. Not anyone in the Fae realm. It must have been the mixture Cymone put together. The combination must have been extra strong."

"No," Cymone said. "I didn't add anything special."

"There had to be. Nothing else makes sense." I shook my head.

Zander peeled my hand off his arm and brought my fingertips to his lips. He pressed gentle kisses on my knuckles. When he spoke, he whispered, "It's not the only answer. You have something special about you, Athena. We've all suspected it for a while."

"But I can't even traverse the leylines smoothly like most elves do."

"Maybe the Gods saw fit to give you other gifts," Zander said.

"Enlighten the human. Is what happened a special elf skill?" Jules asked.

"Occasionally, unique abilities surface," Cymone said. "Athena's mother and grandmother were both gifted healers."

"But they couldn't heal a village with a seismic disturbance. They had to touch each person. Besides, my affinity has always been with the elements and nature. I don't even heal well without help."

"Some healers take on the suffering of their patients and turn it into strength," Cymone said. "I think that is what happened with you today. What were you feeling when it happened?"

"I rubbed the powdered between my hands and placed them on an injured woman," I paused thinking through the events. "Then I asked the earth to help me heal my people."

"Did you feel their pain?"

"In a way. I remember being so angry I swore to rain down the Furies vengeance on Kalypso."

"The anger could have been driven from the hurt you witnessed and might have been enough to supercharge your healing power," Cymone said.

"The shock wave happened when I touched the bloody wounds of the woman," I said. "That seems more like a spell. So, maybe the Furies healed them."

Zander ignored my explanation. "Will it work for all her powers?" His voice returned to normal.

My body relaxed at the sound of it.

"I have no idea," Cymone said.

"The healing caused them pain when the extremities grew back so fast. Normally, it is hours. It doesn't seem like a gift would replace misery with more misery. Those screams were almost as bad as the injured ones."

"There are always consequences," Straton said. "For all choices."

"I think Athena needs to rest," Jules said. "Why doesn't everyone give her some space?" She knew, like she always did, when I slipped into my introverted zone. When the world became too heavy and I just wanted to disappear.

Only I didn't want to disappear this time. I wanted my friends here, and I wanted retribution.

"No, I want everyone to here. Do you mind bringing in some cots and staying? We have revenge to plan."

I didn't miss the looks exchanged. Wrinkled foreheads. Narrowed eyes. Kalypso would meet a fate worse than Hades for this.

THE LAST THING I wanted to do was give a speech, much less a eulogy, for one hundred and three souls. Nausea hit me every time I looked at the list of names. Men, women, and children who would never see their families again, because we decided to bring the war to their doorstep. They never saw Kalypso or her army, and I suspected Zack did the dirty work to regain her favor. His affinity for the earth nearly equaled mine. *Bastard.*

I took my place at the first pyre where the village leader and her husband, at least what remained of them, had been placed. Sorrow blanketed the area and smothered us in grief. Even the trees, flowers and vegetation drooped in a mournful pose. Forest creatures peeked out from the tree line. Dogs, cats, and the other animals stood guard by their deceased companions.

A breeze blew through the bundles of sticks and rattled them in a gentle embrace. I drew in a breath to calm myself.

"As someone who lost both her parents without warning, I know time does not heal the wounds. No words take the pain of their absence away." Sobs echoed through the crowd. The image of my parents and their rule-bending appearance to warn me floated through my mind. *The villages will probably never know a moment so special.* Tears pooled in the corners of my eyes, and I wiped them away. "One thing my parents believed is all life is precious. Their union was meant to be a symbol of solidarity, and this place, your amazing village, was a place of happiness for them and for us as a family. Your kindness and warm welcome will never be forgotten. I pledge to you we will rebuild your village and provide protection."

"And how will you do that?" A familiar voice heckled from the back.

How dare he show himself here. Now. My disgust for him and his choices multiplied.

I exchanged looks with my friends. Zander stiffened into a rigid posture. His face turned to stone. I followed his gaze. *Zack.* He snaked his way alone through the crowd.

"How will you protect these people, Princess, when you let so many die while you hid from our contract?" He gestured to the crowd. "Your promises are empty. The discarded princess, who doesn't even have a throne, who brings pain wherever she goes." He pointed to me. "You couldn't save your parents, Athena, and you can't save these people."

He tried to bait me, but my people deserved better than his disrespect.

I snuck a quick glance at Zander. His skin reddened, and his nostrils flared. His features confirmed my fears. He was about to rain down fury on his brother. Even with the diminished number of elves in the area, I would have a hard time freezing so many people with magick in them. Their resistance would take too much from me. I could freeze Zander alone, but then he would be vulnerable. *Words are what we need now.*

"How dare you show yourself here when your master is accountable for this death and destruction?" I narrowed my eyes at Zack. "When *you* are the one responsible for it?"

The crowd turned on him. The sorrow-saturated air turned hot with anger. My own hatred melted into theirs.

A small twister appeared around him, and he disappeared like Dorothy from Kansas. *Coward.*

"Let the deaths of our friends and family members not feed our anger. Instead, let our sorrow feed our desire to build an inclusive kingdom." *My children will have a place in this world as will anyone else who loves someone outside their designated group. The rest unsaid for now. Revenge will be mine, and it can be said when I defeat Kalypso.*

A whisper left my lips carried by, my friend, Wind. "Aldrnari." The pyres erupted at the same time.

I studied Zander. His nostrils flared. Anger still festered beneath his skin. He looked like he was about to blow. The people didn't need another scene.

I turned to Straton. "Get Zander out of here. He needs a cooling off period."

Straton touched Zander's arm, but Zander shrugged it off. He left without a word.

"How about you?" Jules asked.

"I'm fine. I know where I stand. I've never been more confident, and these people, my people, need me to comfort them right now."

"I'll stay with you. I'm a pretty good comforter." Jules gave me a wink.

"I'll stay too. Straton can handle Zander," Cymone said. "He looked ready to burn everything down to take out Zack."

"Yes, he did," I said.

"He couldn't do that," Jules said. "Could he?"

"He could," I said. "But he wouldn't."

"Some elves have affinity to certain things. Zander's is strength and fire. Zack's is all weather related," Cymone said.

"And Athena?" she asked Cymone.

"I'm right here. You can ask me."

"No offense, but you downplay everything elf related to me," Jules said.

Her remark stung and rightly so. I minimized everything to her. She'd seen so much, and we had to ask for her silence. *The Council might even ask me to wipe her memory once they hear of this, and it might be one of their decrees I ignore.* They dictated the human realm, but not what happened in Lanorinia. It could get tricky.

"Athena's affinities are vast. Her connection to all four elements is strong. Much more than a normal elf, from what we have seen," Cymone said.

"Like the healing yesterday?"

Cymone nodded. "Exactly."

"Enough of this talk," I said. "Our people need our condolences and our love."

CHAPTER 10

My exhaustion stacked on top of my grief, and I wanted to be alone with Zander for a while. I needed his arms around me. I pulled the flap of the tent aside.

Zander paced.

"If you are going to banish me from public, you might as well send me back to Kalypso and her prison," Zander said.

I blinked a few times. "I.." *Ouch.* "Zander, I.."

"I spent five years in confinement." He stopped pacing and faced me. "I will not be a prisoner again."

I rested my hands on either side of his face. Heat radiated off him. I looked him in the eyes. "I didn't think, Zander. I love you, and I will never banish you. I want you by my side as my king."

"As equals, like you told the crowd after my brother left?"

"I wouldn't have it any other way. I'm so sorry. I wanted to prevent a scene for the grieving families. That's all."

"The scene was already made. Do you not trust me?" His voice dripped with bitterness.

"I do, Zander. I do." Tears filled my eyes and spilled down my cheeks. *Just add them to the long line of debt I owed.*

"Maybe, but sending me away hurt, Athena." He took a step back. "Our people needed all of us, and you dismissed me."

"I have faith in you. I promise you I do. I wasn't thinking how it looked or how it made you feel. I wasn't thinking." My heart pounded in my chest. Tears slid down my face.

"I need some time," he said.

"Zander, I didn't mean to hurt you." I reached for him.

He moved a half step out of range. "But you did." He looked me in the eyes and left the tent.

My heart tightened in my chest like pressure from a vise. No sound penetrated the crushing bubble around me. I sank to the ground. *What have I done? I tried to protect everyone and failed to protect my love.*

My body ached from toes to head. Tears flowed in an endless stream of suffering. *I fucked up. And I don't know how to fix it.*

The opening to the tent flapped. "Zander?" I studied through blurry vision.

"Athena, why are you on the floor?" Jules sank down on the ground in front of me. I couldn't make out her face. Everything was a blur. "What's wrong?"

"I hurt Zander," I said.

"You all heal quickly. I think he'll be fine."

A nervous giggle popped out. "No, not like that. I broke his trust," I said.

"What do you mean? You are super trustworthy."

"I didn't trust him enough," I said. "With the Zack disruption earlier."

"Emotions were high for everyone. It's going to be okay." She brushed the hair out of my face with her fingers. "Anyone can see how much he loves you. He'll be back."

"It's the fact I hurt him, Jules. After all he's been through because of me. After all the pain Kalypso inflicted on him because of me, and I sent him away when he wanted to be there for our people."

"I know you're upset," Jules said. "But the Athena I know is strong and confident and would know her man didn't go far. She would know he is out in the yard, training her troops for the big ass freaking fight coming." She cleared her throat. "So, what is really going on here?"

"He's still here? He didn't leave?" The tightness around my heart lessened.

"Yes, training an army fit for a queen." She pointed her finger at me and swirled it around in a circle. "Is there something else bothering you?"

There was something else. It started when my parents pulled me to another realm and appeared as apparitions in front of me. All the distress and grief I'd channeled into being a fighter bubbled to the top now, but I wasn't ready to talk about my parents.

"You're right." I got up from the ground. "A queen wouldn't wallow in pity when her people are suffering."

Jules jumped up next to me. "Well, that's kind of what I meant but not exactly."

"I'm good now. I need to go be with my people and help them. They aren't getting a break from the grief and neither should I."

"You need to wash the snot off your face first," Jules said. She poured some water on a hand towel and handed to me. "Here."

I sat in the chair in front of the vanity and wiped down my face and neck. Jules stood behind me in the mirror with a brush. Each cathartic brush stroke wiped away more of my guilt. Relief washed over me.

"All done." She put the brush down and took the seat next to the table. "You don't have to tell me, but you need to tell someone. And by someone I mean Zander."

"You're right." I twisted my hands. "He's going to be mad when I tell him."

"Sometimes people who love each other get mad. It's okay. But you have to talk about issues to move past them." She put a hand on my knee. "Face facts, Athena. You are not the best communicator."

I pinched the bridge of my nose, but it didn't relieve the pressure built up in my head. "Am I doing the right thing? Do I even belong on the throne?"

"Do you hear yourself? Did you suddenly get diarrhea of the mouth? Kalypso is a fucking tyrant bitch. You owe it to your people, you owe it to your parents, and you owe it to Zander to take that bitch down."

I smiled at her. She motivated me with her passion. "Are you sure you don't want to be queen?"

"I'm only a human. Remember?"

"No, actually. I never think about it anymore." She didn't look like the fragile human I once thought her to be. Her strength inspired me. The way she took on this world, new and strange to her, like she didn't fear a thing. She made me realize I needed to face the truth. Starting with Zander. "Give me a hug. Then I'm going to find my man."

A cool breeze, stronger than the one from this morning, hit me when I left the tent. Dusk peeked over the mountain. I didn't see Zander anywhere. Or Straton. I discovered Cymone showing some villagers how to make medicine.

"Where are Zander and Straton?"

She didn't look up. "They're out patrolling. Sit with us."

The conversation with Zander would be better one-on-one, when he got back.

I dropped down next to them and smiled at the people in the circle.

"Your mother was a gifted healer," an older woman said, as she ground herbs. "Every visit she would spend time with us, making sure we had plenty of medicine. She healed many people in this village."

"I remember some of them. She wanted me to witness the good we did on our trips. I'm sorry my first visit without them couldn't do the same."

"But it has, My Queen," the woman said. "If you hadn't been here, many more would have died."

They don't blame me. A blanket of relief covered me. "You don't think Kalypso would have chosen another location if we hadn't been here?"

"Maybe yesterday, but eventually, she would have come here. We've seen what she has done in other areas."

I reached over and squeezed the woman's hand. She squeezed back and smiled. A genuine smile crossed my face. "Thank you," I said.

"It is us who should be thanking you. You've lost so much, my Queen, all in the name of our protection. You refused to give into Kalypso."

"But I left when everyone else stayed," I said.

"You came back. That's what matters."

"I hope I earn the kindness you have shown me," I said.

"You already have." She worked on her medicine concoction. "Make your sacrifice worth it to you now."

The legacy of my parents lived in this village. The residents' attitudes mirrored the values my parents held true. They lived and breathed the love my parents believed in for the kingdom. All the cities and villages might not feel the same, but the people here inspired me to push forward.

A gentle hand on my shoulder drew my attention up. *Zander.* I grinned. The closeness set off a warmth in me.

His eyes appeared softer and his jaw more relaxed than in the tent.

"Can we talk?"

"Of course."

He extended a hand to help me up. His fingers laced through mine and held on tight. A layer of light perspiration slicked his palm. We walked in silence into the woods. The truth dangled on the end of my tongue, waiting for the right moment. He would hear what my parents told me and what happened that night at the lake.

"We'll have to go deeper if —"

He placed a finger over my lips. "Shh."

We entered a small clearing, where a deer had given birth to two white fawns. A large stag stood watch over the doe and newborns. He showed no fear of us.

Our steps, soundless elf movements, carried us toward them. Zander held out his hand, and I mimicked his movement. The stag stretched his neck towards us and his breath warmed my knuckles as he sniffed us. Approval granted, he once again stood tall. Zander and I knelt down.

"Well done, my lady," I said to the doe. I remembered the apple I'd stashed in my pocket earlier when I walked past the food tent. I offered her the fruit, and she took a bite. The two fawns raised their heads at the crunch. I whispered, "I can't believe they are pure white."

"They are beautiful examples of life. I knew you would want to see them."

"Yes, I'm so glad you did. I thought you were wanting to talk about earlier."

His voice tightened a little. "I do, but we needed this first. To remind us that even in death, there is an opportunity for rebirth."

I stroked the head of a fawn. "And our kingdom needs a rebirth."

CHAPTER 11

Hands entwined, Zander and I walked a short distance until lights shown on a path leading to a clearing. The guards stopped at the opening.

A table covered with a white tablecloth and lit candles waited for us. The soft glow illuminated the darkness. Zander arranged dinner for us in this secluded area. *How did he have time to do this?* Not as private as I would have liked, with the perimeter of guards in view, but they kept to a distance out of elf ear shot.

"Is that pizza on the table?" I asked.

"Yes," Zander said, his face lit by the dancing flames.

"How did you get pizza here?"

"There was an old brick oven that is apparently indestructible." He smiled. "No pepperoni though, only plain cheese."

"I'm good with that." I grinned back. "You must love me to make a pizza." Jules and Zander were the only two who knew of my pizza obsession, but it started with Zander. My smile broadened.

"Oh, I do, and I found some rum too."

"Are you buttering me up?"

He chuckled. "Remember our first date?" His lightness refreshed me.

"Yes, you got someone to traverse us to that pizza place in New York. And they didn't have wine but they had—"

"Rum," Zander finished.

I wrapped my arms around his neck and planted a kiss on his lips.

He pulled back and looked deep into my eyes. His searched mine. "I owe you an apology, Athena. I've been so worried about you and trying to figure out how to protect you." He sucked in a deep breath. "Today I felt like I'd been cast aside. A leftover residual issue I need to deal with from my imprisonment."

"I owe you an apology too. I should have trusted you to think of our people above your hatred for your brother. I took away your choice, and I was wrong."

"I accept your apology, if you accept mine." He kissed the tip of my nose. "But I don't hate my brother. Life would be easier if I did."

For this to be a real apology and to clear the air, I needed to share with him the message from my parents.

"Hold on to accepting my apology. I need to tell you something else."

"You don't have to tell me anything. I trust you."

It stung, knowing I had withheld it from him, but it was my fault for not telling him that night.

"No, I should have told you right away. It happened the night in the woods," I said.

"Which night in the..." He smiled a huge smile. "Oh..."

"Yes, that night." Everything spilled out of my mouth. "My parents froze time and brought me to a different realm."

His brows pinched together. "When you fell down."

"I was returning from their realm."

He nodded.

"They had a message for me."

"What was the message?"

"I had to live. If I die, the Fae die."

"I don't understand," Zander said.

"At first, I didn't either. Then I realized why. I'm the only half elf, half fairy alive."

"But there are lots of half elf, half humans. What does being mixed have to do with anything?"

"Yes, but the others don't have the power you possess. Or Zack for that matter. You two are special. Different, like me. I thought my connections to the four elements were the answer, but now I'm convinced they are. I just can't do this by myself."

"Hmm..." He paused. "It took you long enough to figure out you don't have to defeat her alone."

"I'm sorry I didn't tell you right away. I shouldn't have kept it from you."

"I wish you'd told me, but I understand why you didn't. Your parents are a very special part of you." He pulled me to him and whispered into my hair. "I love you, Athena."

"I love you too," I murmured into his chest. "Can we eat the pizza before it gets cold?"

He chuckled and leaned back.

We gobbled up the small pizza, and one of the guards brought dessert.

"You didn't?" I asked.

"Oh, I did."

The guard placed a funnel cake between us. Something glinted in the middle of the powdered sugar on top. The candle flames danced on the shiny object. I reached for it. "What is that?"

I couldn't remember anything being in the funnel cake on our first date.

Zander leaned closer. "See for yourself."

I wiggled it around and pulled it out. A rectangle-cut emerald sparkled in the candlelight. An emerald represented truth and love. A symbol of a commitment now and in the next life. My mouth dropped open but no words came out. I sucked in a deep breath.

Zander slid out of his chair and onto his knee. He took the ring from me and held my hand. "Athena, you already know you are my one earnest love. Life is incomplete without you. You are the missing half of me. You are the spark that lights the Fae Fire of my heart. Will you marry me?"

Tears pooled in my eyes, but this time for a good reason. *But the contract. The court.* The Seelie and Unseelie court believed in full execution of contracts, regardless of the trickery around them. *Would they try to punish a queen if I beat Kalypso?* No matter what, I'd never marry Zack. Zander was the only man I could make the commitment to. He already had me for eternity.

"What about the contract with Zack?"

"No one will hold you to that after today. Not after what Kalypso did and what you did for the village." He kissed my fingers. "Now, at the risk of asking twice without a response, will you marry me?"

"Yes, of course I will!" I jumped out of my chair and wrapped myself around him. He kissed me and pressed me hard against him.

Excitement tingled through me and tiny sprites danced in the air surrounding us. Their soft lights highlighted us in a softer glow than the candles. Their appearance considered a sign of good luck in our legends, but it was the first time I'd seen so many. I held out my hand and one fluttered to my palm. She crossed her closed fists over her chest and inclined her head to me. Respect--even harder to earn from them. I inclined my head in return towards the beautiful sprite. She opened her hands and widened them towards Zander and me. Bits of light danced around us like sparklers without the burn.

"It's so beautiful. Thank you," I said.

She fluttered off to join the others.

"Such a gift," Zander said.

I beamed at him. "It is." I draped my arm lazily around his neck.

"I meant you."

A blush rose in my cheeks. "You flatter me, my love."

"I speak the truth," he paused. "My love."

"Whoa," Jules said from behind me.

I smiled. "Did you invite them?" I whispered.

Zander nodded.

"Good choice."

The sprites buzzed our friends.

"Congratulations, my Queen, and our future king." Straton said. "Such a great blessing from the sprites."

"Thank you, Straton," I said. "It is indeed."

Zander and I untangled to accept the well wishes from our group..

"Congratulations, Athena." Cymone hugged me and turned to Zander. "I knew you would ask her at the absolute worst time."

Zander laughed her comment off with a shrug.

"You knew about this?" I cocked my head toward Cymone.

"You don't think he could have pulled this all off alone, do you?" she asked.

"Don't let her fool you. She tried to talk him out of proposing tonight, but then one of these little light thingies showed up." The sprite who had lit on my hand buzzed in Jules' face. "We know. You're beautiful little blessings. Blah blah." The sprite zapped her on the nose and flew away.

"You don't want to be on the bad side of a sprite. They might be little, but they can channel enough electrical current to power a small city," I said.

Jules hugged me and whispered in my ear. "Are you sure you

want to marry him? Doesn't it mean you would have to live here full time?"

I whispered in return. "I'm sure I want to marry him, and we'll see on the other issue. Until I appoint someone else, I'm technically still a council member, which means I have to be there when the Council is in session. Is there something else you're worried about?" I pulled back. Jules' life wasn't here. She would have to go back, and I would have to make a decision on protection for her in the human realm.

"Would a human be allowed to visit you here, or will there be some kind of vampire mind wipe when I leave? I don't want to forget my best friend." Jules wiped at her eyes. She understood the stakes better than I realized.

I squeezed her to me. "I promise you, no vampire mind wipes. We don't need them to do it anyway." I smiled at her.

Her face dropped. "What? Vampires are real too?"

"Probably not like in your stories, but yes, they are out there."

Zander slid a hand around my waist and pulled me to his side. "Don't get her started on vampires. She has a thing for them. Her boyfriend before me was one."

"Don't believe him. I kissed a vampire on a diplomatic trip with my father to Enchanted Rock. Nothing more than a kiss, and I didn't even like it."

Laughter rolled up from the group and the sprites danced around us.

Even in this wonderful moment, I wondered what tomorrow would bring. The sprite's blessing didn't guarantee we would defeat Kalypso, or that Zander and I would both live to see our wedding date. Zack remained at large, and his power endangered everyone we involved. His abilities afforded him sneak attacks, and my friends distracted me enough I missed the signs too many times. Doubt crept into my mind. Doubt in our ability to win, and doubt in my myself.

Is risking their lives worth ensuring my own carried on? What if my parents were wrong? Their conviction exceeded my own confidence in my abilities. *Failure was not an option. Their message said as much.*

I'd never wanted something more, nor been so unsure if I was doing the right thing.

My heart raced. The world spun. Lights danced in front of me, and it wasn't the sprites. *Or was it?* The darkness of the night closed in around me until no light remained. *What the...* I blinked several times, but there was no light to adjust to. *Am I blind?* I blinked a few more times. *Shit. Am I?* I slid into an unknown territory, unable to get my bearings. Nothing but black engulfed me and distorted my ability to balance. I stumbled around in a circular pattern. My feet bumped against something solid on the ground. My toe caught and I pitched forward. My fingers dug into gravel. I'd been sent to a cave of some sort. My head struck against a rock, and I reached up to the spot. Nothing appeared wet, other than the damp smell of the cave. My eyes refused to stay open. One name crossed my mind as everything went cold.

Kalypso.

CHAPTER 12

A heaviness pressed on my chest. The part of my back previously stabbed by Zack's short blade throbbed like a fresh wound. I blinked until my eyes adjusted to the light. *Light. Not blind.* The ache in my head threatened to split my skull open. "Help me." My voice barely came out as a whisper. The weight on me grew heavier. I raised my head against the agony in my back.

Horror gripped me. I swallowed a scream. It stuck on a knot in my throat. *Snakes. Tons of snakes.* Snakes pinned me to the ground like I was staked. I lowered my head in slow motion and closed my eyes tight. "Help me." My words came out more normal this time. "Help me." Snakes couldn't sense fear, but they could smell the hormonal change from fear and react to the nervousness. *Calm. I have to stay calm.*

This could not get any worse.

"They will not let us approach, Athena," Zander said. His voice sounded distant.

I gritted my teeth when I wanted to scream. *Thank the Gods I'm not alone.* "What do you mean?"

"We think they're enchanted," Cymone said.

"Get these snakes off me," I ground out.

Screams came from the direction of the group. I couldn't see what happened. Fear strangled me worse than the snakes. My friends couldn't help me, and I couldn't help them. A tear dropped from the corner of my eye. Fae tears came at a cost. Always.

The snakes hissed. A strange growl noise and hot breath touched my face. *Good Gods. What now?* I opened my eyes. A giant lizard thing looked me in the eye. I held my breath and fought the urge to do a backstroke out of there. *Not that I could move.* I'd seen one of these before. They'd been extinct on Earth for a long time, but in Lanorinia they had lived longer. Still, they roamed this area well before my lifetime. *A velociraptor? What crazy nightmare is this?*

The velociraptor's jaws opened. I squeezed my eyes shut and braced for razor-like teeth. The beast let out a few low growls and a few chomps. Drops of liquid hit my face. *No pain.* I peeked through one eye. The dinosaur devoured several snakes in brutal fashion. I stayed glued in place, afraid I would be the next course. It looked at me with recognition. *Those eyes.* He continued to make a meal of the snakes.

All the snakes eaten, the creature stopped next to me. Blood dripped from its mouth. He lowered his head to my face. Snake flesh wedged between his sharp teeth. Hot huffs tickled my cheek. *Gods. Please don't let me die by velociraptor.* A familiar smell hit me. *A shifter. I know this shifter. But he's an elf. How?*

I sat up in place. "Straton?"

The velociraptor roared and escaped down a cave passage.

"Was that Straton?" I turned to where my friends' voices had come from, but no one was there. *This isn't real.*

The darkness rippled around me.

"This isn't real," I said out loud. *Kalypso is pulling a mind trick on me.*

Laughter echoed all around me. "More than a trick, dear Athena."

"Get out of my head." My body tensed, which pissed me off, because she possibly knew it.

"Then you'll be all alone," she said. "Is that what you want?"

"If you're my only choice for company, then solitude is welcome."

"As you wish." A twinge marked her exit.

Kalypso preferred punishing in person. There were two things she needed to invade a mind with Unseelie dark magick. The first was to know the person whose mind she wanted to breach, and the second was blood. *The knife in my back from Zack. Literal and physical.*

Since she chose to raid my head, she must not have my body. Which only left one question. *Where in Hades is my body? Is it still in the village?*

The last thing I remembered was laughing about kissing some random vampire. *Why is this so fuzzy?* I was with my friends in a field. *Zander.* Zander and I had dinner, and he proposed. I looked down at my hand. *No ring. Because you are in your own mind, stupid.* I glanced again, and the emerald ring glimmered. *That's Much better. I'm in control here.*

"Wake up," I told myself. "Wake up."

"Wake up, wake up, wake up."

"Wake up!"

Fuck. This is going to be harder than I thought.

I studied my mind cave. *Why a cave? I thought it would be more colorful.*

Hhhmm. I walked in the dim light to what appeared to be the outlet, but it was a dead end.

"The bitch locked me away in a corner of my mind somehow."

How do I get out of here?

"Wake the fuck up!"

Maybe if I go to sleep, I'll wake up unstuck. I laid down on the hard cave floor and closed my eyes.

Sleep didn't come. Not then or the half dozen other times I tried. I stood up and studied the cave. Clearly, Kalypso did this to drive me mad. *And it's working.* I paced around in a circle and contemplated the different ways I could take her head.

My elf was my dominant side. My fairy magick made rare appearances. My sides were meant to be equal, but like many hereditary traits, it just didn't work like that. Fairy magick created a lot of sleep remedies, so maybe my fairy side could wake me up. *Worth a shot.*

I imagined wings on my back. The wings grew in strength, until they built up enough power to lift me. I imagined them lifting me through the roof, and light broke through the top. I flapped the wings and launched towards it. My wings carried me to the opening, and I rocketed out the hole.

Colors everywhere. *That's more like it.* Meadows, creeks, and forests covered the land as far as I could see. It might have been what I willed from the cave, but it was beautiful. My body relaxed.

Let's try this again. "Wake up, Athena."

The scenery fragmented in a kaleidoscope style.

I blinked until my eyes adjusted to the light.

"She's coming around." Jules voice came from a distance.

A warm hand slipped into mine. "My love."

"What happened? Did Kalypso attack us again?" I looked around to see my and Zander's tent.

"No attacks. How do you feel?"

"Why does my entire body hurt?" I asked. "Help me sit up."

Zander pulled me into a seated position. He and Jules hovered over me.

The pain in my back throbbed. "Did I get stabbed in the back again?"

Zander and Jules exchanged a look.

"Just tell me."

"We need to show you." Zander stood and held out a hand to me. He pulled me to my feet. He and Jules walked me to the mirror.

Fairy wings extended out from my shoulder blades. My knees buckled. Zander held me up. Pastel iridescence danced over them. "They're beautiful."

"It appears you earned your fairy wings." His reflection smiled at mine in the mirror.

"But fairies are born with them. I've never heard of this."

"Maybe you're a late bloomer." Jules said. "Or maybe your body saved them for when you needed them most."

"Let's pretend it's the latter," I said. "What am I supposed to do with these things? Not being born with wings, I never paid any attention to the discussions around them." I extended them out to their full length.

"We'll figure it out," Zander said. "But let's get you back in bed to rest."

"I actually feel pretty good. So, did they just pop out while I was locked in my own head?" I looked at them in the mirror. "How long was I out?

"Something like that," Zander said. "And you were out for a few hours."

"He's being nice. You made some really weird growling noises, and then you sat up. They poked through your shirt. Then you fell back on the bed," Jules said.

"I had a strange dream," I said. *Was it all just a dream? It sure felt real.* I remembered Kalypso's voice. "It wasn't a dream. Kalypso locked me in a coffin size part of my mind, and I'm not sure why."

"Cymone suspected it might be some Unseelie magick holding you there," Zander said. "Pretty powerful magick to get to you while awake instead of asleep."

"She had my blood from the knife. It's the only way she could,"

I said. "Luckily, it probably took it all to do that, so she shouldn't be able to do it again."

"Your wings are beautiful." He ran his hand lightly over the edge.

"Wonder what the elves are going to say about these things?" I extended them out and flapped once. The force stirred a decent breeze. *Impressive. And fun.* "I want to try them out."

Cymone walked in with Straton on her heels. "Rest first. Fly later," she said.

"The great thing about being a queen? I don't need anyone's permission." I smiled and flapped my wings a couple of times.

Cymone grabbed her forehead. "Can you for once listen?"

"I'm teasing, but I really do feel fine."

I climbed into bed to satisfy them all. Made sure my head faced away from my friends, so they couldn't see my eyes were open.

"Zander, Straton and I have something to show you." Cymone's voice drifted over my shoulder.

"I don't want to leave her right now. Can it wait?"

"She'll be fine," Cymone said.

"I'll get a pitcher of fresh water and some food. Then I can wait here with her until you get back," Jules said.

I closed my eyes.

Zander pressed his lips against my temple.

Why did these wings come now? I never thought about my fairy side, and after my mother's death, the fairy side of the family didn't visit much. Even though my parents' marriage and my birth were supposed to heal the strain between fairies and elves, the truth is the two events didn't. They both were strong and power hungry in the ruling class, and neither of them treated the rest of the Fae with much respect.

I rolled over to an empty room. Everyone left, and I never heard a sound.

I hopped to my feet. My wings unfolded out to my sides. *I shouldn't. It couldn't hurt to just try them out for a minute.* In my youth, the elves would comment on how lucky I was to look more elf than fairy. The anguish in my mother's eyes crushed me then. The wish I asked the universe for most often was to be equal parts my father and mother. The wings physically answered that wish.

The tent door flapped like an invitation. I peered around and didn't see a soul. *Strange. No guard posted nearby.* I knew better, but to be able to celebrate a piece of my mother called to me. It was important I do it alone the first time. The sun's position in the sky told me everyone would be at breakfast. *I was out longer than I thought.* With the forest in sight, I snuck through the last possible place for exposure in the village.

Just a quick try to see how strong they are. I straightened my spine and turned my eyes upward. My wings unfolded, and I examined each one. *How hard can flying be? Time to see.* One powerful flap and my wings propelled me into the air. They pushed the air down and sent me soaring higher. Adrenaline pounded through my body. The sheer freedom exhilarated me. All the weight of commitments and duties sat on the ground. *Zander would love this. Would I be able to bring him with me?* My wings certainly seemed strong enough to carry someone.

Zing. The noise rang out to my left. I pulled up to hover in my current location. *Zing.* My shoulder burned and ached. I looked towards it and saw blood pooled on my shirt. *Zing.* My wing ripped in two. Agony spidered out, and I tumbled towards the earth over a clearing. No trees to ask to cradle the fall. *This is it. I'm sorry, Zander.* The descent took longer than I expected, but the ground grew closer with each passing moment. *No healer nearby. The impact would be too much.* The grassy area came into focus. There, in the middle of the green space, stood Zander. My eyes closed. *I don't know how he's here, but thank the gods.*

He caught me with ease.

But something felt off. He touched me wrong.

"Give it to her now," he said.

I forced my eyes open. "Zack," I hissed.

"Yes, it's me."

My eyes drooped. *Drugged me.* My speech slurred. "Just wait, Zack."

CHAPTER 13

Stings against my cheek woke me up. "Get up, Athena."
My eyes' reluctance to open mirrored my reluctance to acknowledge the situation. The fuzzy shape came in to focus. A hand tried to strike me again, but I threw my arm up to block it. "Kalypso." Nausea roiled through me, and I threw up at her feet.

She stepped back. "I told you the proper dose to give her. You've poisoned her," she chastised the person next to her.

Black boots. I glanced up to see Zack. My body expelled vomit at him.

They deserve it. If I didn't already feel like death, I'd laugh.

"Clean her up. We need her in an hour." She turned her back to me. "And clip those wings. There's a reason we suppressed her fairy side."

Questions teetered on my tongue. *Wings? Suppressed? Why? How?* I refused to give her the satisfaction of my curiosity.

Fingers clutched my chin. "We're finally going to honor our marriage contract," Zack said.

I wrenched my face away. My thumb rubbed the ring finger. I glanced down to find my ring missing.

"Zander's ring is being returned to him."

I forced myself to not react. I tried to be stone like. Inside a piece of me died.

"When he comes for you, you will tell him your place is here."

"Why should I do that?"

"Because your friends will die, Zander will die, and we will destroy village after village until you agree."

"It'll never happen," I said. "Zander is more than capable of stopping you." The putrid odor of my own vomit wafted towards me. I gagged and coughed.

Zack scooted a bucket in front of me with his foot. Splatter from my previous expulsions dotted his boots. "I thought your people meant more to you than that, Athena. You saw how easily I destroyed the village you thought would protect you."

He doesn't know. He can't know about the healing. But he did know about the engagement. Just because of the ring? My options were pretty weak. If I said no, not one thread of doubt existed about his ability to kill as many innocent people as he needed to in order to convince me. If I said yes, then I would save lives. When I first came back to Lanorinia, I didn't think I could offer much to my people. I just wanted to save my love. Now, the chance to save all of them dangled in front of me. *Did it really matter if the way to get there looked different than I pictured?* I'll find a way to kill Kalypso and Zack, no matter the cost to me.

"Fine, Zack. If I have your word they will all be safe. I want your promise though." An elf promise was an agreement bound by blood. If broken, the severity determined the punishment. If he hurt or killed them, he could suffer the same.

"I'll make that promise when you marry me," he said.

"Then at least promise on your brother, as a good faith gesture." Elves so rarely agreed to it. I wasn't sure if it held the same strength for a half-elf, but Seelie and Unseelie alike upheld it.

"If you marry me, I promise not to harm Zander." He turned to the maids with eyes downcast. "Get her ready."

~

THE LACK of discomfort in my back from the clipped wings disturbed me. I'd only had them a short time, but Kalypso took part of me, a precious part from my mother. Between the poison Zack gave me and whatever they knocked me out with, it must have dulled the nerves there. The dress fit so tight, the gown should be rubbing against the fresh wounds. A skilled healer could have been sent while I was out cold, but I couldn't imagine Kalypso being kind to me. The reflection in the mirror looked like me, but wasn't.

Not exactly the wedding dress I pictured for myself. Or the groom. Zack and Kalypso planned to put me on display. This giant, layered dress looked like a cupcake. I hated it. As if I needed more proof on how little Kalypso and Zack knew me, the outfit looked like a ridiculous movie prop. My tastes were much simpler, and a skirt with seven layers poofed out in a bell shape didn't make the cut. My only comfort was Zander wouldn't see me in the hideous thing.

I paced the length of my former room, which now served as my cell. The heavy gown weighed me down, but I trudged back and forth. With the poison purged from my system, my faculties returned. They had filled the room with Elfin roses. Any other day I would have loved them, but not today. Today the sweet, floral scent assaulted my nostrils. Vomit threatened at every whiff. *Gods! How could I have been so stupid?* My pace slowed. *How did Zack know I had wings and would be able to fly?*

The door swung open wide. Zack walked through. "Wedding time."

My mouth dried like I'd swallowed cotton balls. A tightness settled deep in my chest. I took a step back towards the window.

"If you jump, our deal is off," Zack said, like he read my mind. "Your friends will die. My brother will die."

Suck it up. I took a step forward. My life lost any importance at the thought of others dying for me to live. This exchange offered freedom for them. Zander survived imprisonment for five years. I could survive this.

Zack led us down the hall. Each window we passed teased me with escape. Escape meant the destruction of everything I loved. Everything my parents built would die. No way out. My chest clenched even tighter, so tight I thought I might implode. *Not an option.* If I imploded, everyone died. If I do anything other than what Kalypso and Zack want, everyone dies. Me, my life, enslaved to them from here until I found a way to defeat them.

We made the corner. "This isn't the way to the Grand Ballroom."

"No, we're going to the Processional Balcony."

I planted my feet and stepped back. *No way in Hades am I doing this facing the city. My people will not see me submit to Zack or Kalypso. Not without knowing the truth.*

"Do you want everyone to die, Athena? Really?" he asked.

Kalypso's voice drifted over my shoulder. "Come now, Athena. Your friends await."

I drew my chin over my shoulder and skewered her with my eyes.

"They are waiting on you," she said. Her smile contorted to an evil sneer.

Dread pounded through me with every beat of my heart. A dull roar from the crowd below drifted to us. The doors opened, and the wind carried the sweet aroma of the Elfin Roses to me. Nausea hit with a wave of memories of the day my father died on the balcony, and I leaned over a planter to expel what little there was left in my stomach. My eyes teared up from the force. I straightened and turned back. *At least I will taste like vomit for the wedding kiss. A small satisfaction.*

Zack pulled a handkerchief from his pocket, dabbed the corners of my eyes, and wiped my mouth. I pulled away from him. He handed the fabric to a guard. "Get her a glass of water." The guard took a few steps away to a pitcher on a table in the hall. He brought me a glass of cool water and waited.

As I drank, I contemplated who and how many I could take out with broken glass. I needed to see my friends and Zander first to know they were okay. *Plan aborted.*

Kalypso stepped onto the balcony and walked to the edge. The crowd grew silent in her presence. Zack took my hand again and pulled me with him. I peered over the edge, but didn't see Zander or my friends. The crowd erupted in applause. Their cheers crested over me like a wave. I focused on the chants. My heart warmed. Their cheers strengthened my desire to save the kingdom. "Queen Athena." The chant rang out, over and over. *Kalypso won't like this.*

She held out her hand and the crowd quieted. "We have some wonderful news, my people."

I snorted.

Kalypso cut her eyes at me.

Zack squeezed my hand in painful reassurance.

"The rumors are true. Princess Athena has returned to us."

I sucked in to keep from snorting again. My gaze shot to the raised platform on the promenade below the balcony. There, above the crowd but out of reach from the balcony, stood Straton, Cymone, Jules, and Zander. I closed my eyes to hold the tears inside. Kalypso put them close enough to witness everything but too far for them to hear me speak. I met Zander's eyes. My first instinct was to say I love you to him, but death would be the outcome if I did. He'd die for me, and I'd die for him. *There's no winning for you here today. Please Gods. Please deliver my message to him.* Telepathy wasn't my gift, so prayers were all I had.

"She's served us on the North American Council at Enchanted Rock for the last five years, and she has decided to relinquish her seat to her husband. Well, he will be after today. This will allow her to remain in Lanorinia full time."

The crowd clapped and cheered my name.

"She has decided, in the best interest of Lanorinia, that I will remain your queen." If she expected cheers like they did for me, she got none. My people stood silent at her proclamation.

They wanted something I couldn't give them today. Kalypso's power would grow. My emotions weren't in check, and my magick bled out. Energy crackled at my fingertips.

Zack dropped my hand.

It dawned on me I might have an option. The only option really. I could stop her today.

I'm sorry, Mom and Dad. I can't be as good as you. My gaze locked on Zander's. I mouthed, "I'm sorry. I love you." Even from here I could see the torment on his face, the redness of his eyes. He knew what I knew. Only one option left. Tears spilled from mine. *Elf tears always have a cost. I'll pay the price today.* He mowed over the guards in front of the platform, but I'd already reached out to the elements. *Wind. Fire. Water. Earth.*

The energy built into a purplish-blue hue at my hands. I stepped back slightly and bowed my head. The tears splashed against the pulsing current around my hands. My lifeforce melded with the elements. The skies grew dark overhead and thunder vibrated everything around us.

Today is my day. I'm ready.

I raised my head and looked Kalypso in the eye. My protective bubble slammed down around us. Everyone on the outside safe. The energy of the Gods coursed through me. I commanded intense wattage. My hair tingled and stood on end. The stink of burnt hair filled the area inside the shield. Lightning descended from the sky at my command able to pass through the invisible protection. I met it with the electricity in my hands and thrust the energy toward Kalypso. Black smoke erupted. A crack snaked out at her feet. The balcony collapsed beneath us. *This is it.* I lost sight of the others. My body tumbled to the ground amid the rubble. My concentration centered on keeping the bubble around the wreckage. Trapped her like a rat.

Today we are all free.

The impact knocked my breath out of me. Intense pain rocketed through my legs, my back, my arms, and my skull. My lifeforce drained. I couldn't maintain the protection. The bubble burst. Broken pieces of the balcony piled on top of me. The weight crushed me against the debris underneath. Dust burned my throat. My ears rang. The sound pierced my head. And then hollow silence.

Today I chose my people, my friends, and my love.

Today I rest on the Great Hill.

Today I see my parents again.

CHAPTER 14

*D*eath *is silent.* The quiet unnerved me. The one thing I counted on in death was seeing my parents, but it was dark and silent. Humans believed in purgatory. Fae had no place to purify their souls between lives. We moved on to our next phase, but this place resembled what the stories of purgatory sounded like.

Death is lonely. My parents arrived together when they pulled me to their dimension, but no one greeted me at my death. I didn't fulfill my destiny, so I'm being punished. I stopped Kalypso. *Doesn't that count?* Apparently, extra credit doesn't count towards karma.

Death sucks. I fucked up enough I get to spend my next life alone. *Without Straton's infuriating formality and unwavering loyalty. Without Cymone's guidance and sister-like love. Without Jules' chastising and fearlessness.* The part which disheartened me the most was a life without Zander. *His touch. The feel of his lips on mine. His support and unconditional love.*

A small white light appeared in front of me. *Mother? Father? They came for me.* The light increased to a size too large for a sprite. The airy figure formed into my mother. Warmth spread over me and light radiated from me. She smiled, but sadness settled in the corners of her eyes.

"Mother," I beamed. "I wondered how to get to you."

"I found you." She touched an ethereal hand to my face, the gesture soft and warm, almost like a corporeal touch.

"I can feel you." I laid my hand over hers. "Is Father coming?"

"No," she said. The sadness deepened and creased her face.

"Where's Father?"

"All actions have consequences, Athena."

"Where is Father?" A nervous twitch flitted across my spine.

"He is answering for our interference."

"Because you warned me, but I died anyway." A pain spiked in the back of my throat. I failed them, and he paid the price.

"Not our visit earlier. This one." She cocked her head to the side, like I should know what she meant.

"I don't understand. I died."

"But you have to go back, Athena, and we are sending you back."

"I want to stay here with you," I said. The years without them left me lost. "You and Father." Back in Lanorinia, my friends waited. Zander waited. I looked for somewhere to sit down, but there were no chairs. *A quiet place to think. That's what I need.*

"It's not your time." She brushed her fingers across my cheek through my tears. "Elf tears always come at a cost."

"Even here?"

"Even here," she said. "Your tears, your father's tears." She opened her other hand which held a few drops in it and mixed them with the ones she'd wiped from my face. "Fairy tears have a price too, but they also have power." She wiped a finger under her eye and released it in the small pool on her hand.

"Mother, let me stay for a little while."

"You still have much to do, and the longer you stay, the harder it is to leave," she said. "It won't be easy, but you must fight for it.

Remember how much we love you, and remember your destiny. Be the change your Father and I began."

She flipped her wrist. The liquid slipped from her hand and glistened like stardust. Our tears held together on the way to my feet.

"I love you, Mom."

Her sad smile deepened. "I love you."

The liquid surrounded my feet like melted snow. The familiar pull of a leyline traversed me through on a route I didn't know. My mind forgot the trail as it passed. *The living shall not have a path to the dead.* A piece of a Fae poem traced from my memories. *Not easily anyway.*

The ringing in my ears returned. Misery and agony racked my body. My eyes wouldn't open. The anguish not like any I'd ever suffered.

Cymone's voice floated from what seemed like half a world away. "Zander, she's gone."

A wail rebounded around me.

The torment consumed like flesh on hot coals. My eyes wouldn't open, but a tear squeezed out the side. *Always a cost.*

A finger traced the tear along my temple. "Athena, fight. Fight like you do. Fight with everything you have," Zander whispered. His breath tickled my ear. "Cymone, she's alive. Get some healers over here now."

My head pounded. It seemed ready to crack open at the next sound. Retreat beckoned. Retreat to the place free of pain. The path lost on my return. *No.* My parents paid a price for my restoration. *Fight. Mother told me to fight.* I reached for my inner strength.

Zander whispered, "Athena, can you hear me?"

Nothing cooperated in my body. My toes, my legs, my hands, my arms, my eyes. None of them responded to my request. Not even my mouth or voice.

"Her breaths are ragged. She's barely with us." Cymone's voice fractured my thoughts.

Fight. My body jerked and spasmed out of control. Fresh pain spread out up and down my spine. *Mother, why did you send me back to this? I'd let go. I don't know if I can stand this.*

"You move there," Cymone said. "And you there." *Where is there?* "Straighten her leg."

New pain shot through my extremities as hands placed pressure all over me.

"Do not stop until I tell you." Cymone's voice commanded full of authority.

My aches and throbs of agony subsided. A finger complied with my request to move. *Fight.* The word refused to make sound. Every inch of my body weighted down in comparison to the lightness of death, but the discomfort diminished. My breaths came easier. I coughed against the dust still in my lungs.

"Stop," I whispered. I didn't want them to take all the aches. I needed reminders to keep my memories intact.

"We're almost done," Cymone whispered.

"Stop." My voice grew. "Stop now."

All the hands fell away, but the presence of bodies remained close.

My eyes hurt, but they answered my attempt to open them.

"Athena," Zander whispered in my other ear. "Thank the Gods."

"Help me up." My voice sounded full of gravel.

Zander helped me to a seated position. Broken remnants of the balcony surrounded me. Rain pelted down on us. I hadn't noticed the dampness before. A glance around revealed everyone was soaked, including me. The stubborn, sore muscles protested every movement I made. *Good. I won't forget.*

"We thought you were lost," Zander said, his voice soft. Softer than I ever remembered. He brushed the hair off my face.

"Please tell me no innocents were hurt."

"Not one. Except you."

I'm no innocent. My parents are paying for my mistakes. "Thank goodness. And at least Kalypso is dead."

Zander sighed. "Not exactly."

"What do you mean?" *She fell with me. I killed myself for nothing. My parents sent me back for nothing.* I saw her fall with me. I held her inside the bubble with me to make sure.

"She rescued Zack, and they fled."

"How?"

"She was near death. When I saw you, I wanted her to suffer, so I left her." He shook his head. "When I looked over my shoulder, I saw one of her guardsmen tending to her. A healer, apparently, because he saved her. She then saved Zack."

"Gods dammit!"

"Easy, my love. You received a blessing today. Don't be damning things."

"And I don't think they are going to let me back either."

His forehead bunched up. "What do you mean?"

"Nothing," I said. *How do I tell him, my one love, I'm pretty sure I'll not be welcomed back to the next life?* "So, Kalypso will be back and nothing changed. You should have made sure she was dead versus saving me."

"Your people chose to save you over Kalypso. They made their choice. I would make the same choice again, and I think it's safe to say they would too. You are their queen."

Jules' face came into focus where Cymone had been. Mud and blood caked on her. She followed my eyes. "It's not mine." She squeezed my fingers. "Look around. Look at the people."

I released her hand and looked past her. Tears pooled in my eyes, and I held them in. *My people.* My people kneeled. As far as I could see, my people kneeled to me.

"Help me to my feet." I held my hands out. Always there to

support me, Cymone, Straton, Jules, and Zander. They helped me upright. Zander supported me with a tight hold around my waist.

"Rise."

They stood.

I wobbled.

Zander's gripped tightened, and Jules slid to my other side to brace me.

"We bow for no one in Lanorinia." I looked into the eyes of my people.

They exchanged looks. My voice was too weak to carry to everyone.

Gentle Wind, carry my words to my people. "We bow for no one. We are strong. We are love. We are Lanorinia."

The chant started small. "Long live Queen Athena."

With each repetition it grew. "Long live Queen Athena."

I held a hand up in a gesture not unlike the one Kalypso raised a short time ago.

"My father was a great king of Lanorinia and my mother a great queen. The joining of their elf and fairy blood was not what made them great. The love of Lanorinia and the people are what made them our greatest leaders. Today, I repeal the laws which prevent elves and fairies from marrying or sharing a home. Love who you love, Lanorinia."

Zander's fingers dug into my bruised ribs.

I winced.

"The Seelie and Unseelie court will not like the repeal," he whispered for only me.

I refused to whisper, but I kept my voice low enough the crowd wouldn't hear. "Fuck the court. They are next on my list. Death made me realize I have a homeland, and I'm taking it back to build the place my parents envisioned."

"Your people seem to support it," Jules said. Her free hand grabbed mine.

I squeezed.

"I think your parents would too," Zander said.

My head tilted up towards him. "I know they would."

He kissed my forehead.

"It's not going to be easy."

"It never is with you, Athena."

I laughed. "The Gods know I'm going to do everything the hard way first."

Zander snorted. "That they do. Let's get you inside. You have a kingdom to rule."

"No, I have a kingdom entrusted to me, and I'm going to lead them to brighter days."

I gave Straton instructions to share with the people and a promise to visit the city tomorrow.

Cymone stayed by his side.

A genuine smile spread across my lips. *I have a homeland. I have my friends. I have my love.*

One single word drifted across the wind. *Today.*

CHAPTER 15

1 *Month Later*

MY FAMILY INSIGNIA and crests restored, the palace appeared more normal. The throne felt like dress up, like it belonged to my father still. Zander suggested I use my mother's, but I chose to keep my father's. Even as some traditions changed, some needed to remain.

We'd performed a dozen marriages between elves and fairies since my proclamation. Many had lived in hiding, and some of the couples already had children. *Kids who shared a common bond with me.* Not being one-of-a-kind made Lanorinia warmer to me, like when my parents were alive.

"A messenger from the North American Council sent this." Zander held out the folded paper with the NAC seal on it.

I refused all requests from the North American Council to send a representative, but they continued to send an invitation every few days. "You know my answer. As the King of Lanorinia, you can answer as well as me."

"I'm not king yet, and they want to hear from you."

I took the paper from him and unfolded it. I reread it three times. "Did you send someone to the Council?"

Zander's brows pinched together. "You know I wouldn't without consulting you."

I handed the paper back to him. I'd hoped for more time before they made a move, but the note dashed it.

His forehead wrinkled into a tight bunch. "Who?"

"I have no idea how, but I have two guesses."

"Kalypso and Zack."

"It has to be Zack, but I bet Kalypso is pulling the strings. Regardless, there is only one way to find out who is impersonating a representative of Lanorinia."

"We need to go there," he said.

It still pissed me off the way the North American Council agreed to Kalypso's terms five years ago, and I had only been back when required since then. They hadn't listened to me then, and I didn't know if they would listen now. I refused to let Kalypso maintain any power. Swift actions to block her had to be taken.

"It will probably be a fight. No telling what lies they are spinning for the NAC."

"We should take the guards with us."

I nodded my agreement. "Do you think we should postpone the wedding?"

He wrapped his arms around me, holding me close. "Cold feet already?"

"Not now. Not ever." I laced my fingers behind his neck.

"Good to know." He kissed my forehead. "Your people are really looking forward to the wedding."

"Just my people?"

"I'm looking forward to making you my wife." Zander pressed his lips to mine.

"Tomorrow *our* people will meet their future king and my future husband." The words sounded so sweet. "Today we need to make sure we are keeping their kingdom secure." The word 'today' hung heavy in the air, the taste bitter on my tongue.

"I'll send a couple of guardsmen through to prepare for our arrival. We can go as soon as they advise." He went to make the arrangements.

The urge to go alone ate at me, but I wouldn't do it. Not this time. My selfish need to fix things on my own nearly cost me my family, my friends, and Zander. I died because of it. My parents paid a price to send me back, and I still didn't know the cost. I might never know. A piece of me stayed dead from it. I couldn't tell Zander. *How could I tell him I was no longer whole?* Some part of me remained in the next life. *After the wedding.* I repeated the phrase to myself so many times over the last month when I thought of telling him. *After the wedding* became almost as dreaded to me as the word *today*.

Whatever time I had in Lanorinia, I vowed to spend it making up my mistakes to my people, my friends, and my future husband.

I sat on the throne. The throne that had been my father's. The throne now mine. A warmth came over me like a hug from my parents. *I'm home.* I had a family, and we were safe today.

Today, I am in Lanorinia.
Today, I am the queen.
Today, I am ready.

The End...
For Now

ACKNOWLEDGMENTS

Group projects make me cringe in general. I am scarred by them from college. Enchanted Rock Immortals has not been without its challenges, but it has been fiercely rewarding working with my talented critique partners and friends to bring this world to life. When one of us faced a bout of imposter syndrome or other obstacles, the others were there to pick our friend up. Everyone deserves friends who lift each other up.

I am incredibly proud of the novellas each of my friends has created. As most who know me will say, I'm a witch and vampire kind of girl, so writing the Fae Clan novella was a new adventure for me, and I love it as I love the other clans the group created. I put my heart in it just like my writing sisters did in theirs. Amanda, Eve, Fenley - you ladies are truly talented, and the stories in the box set show how much. Robin, I'm glad you stuck with us and cannot wait for your first novella to be out in 2021! Thank you all for being such wonderful writing partners.

To my editor, Dawn, thank you for your patience and understanding of my characters and the world. You are a gift!

Thank you to my family and friends, and the world of support they have shown for me at all times. My mom, my sister, and my nieces have listened to ideas, read blurbs and books, and cheered me on this journey. I could not have made it this far without them. And to my dad, who I promised to publish before he passed away, I know you would be proud, but I haven't forgotten about the one you wanted to see in print. I love you all!

ABOUT THE AUTHOR
SUSAN PERSON

Susan Person is a multi-contest finalist in the paranormal and dark paranormal categories. A member of Romance Writers of America since 2013, she has been a PRO since 2015 and was a 2018 and 2019 member of the PRO Steering Committee. Recently, she returned to college to pursue a degree in anthropology and will graduate in 2021. Susan enjoys meeting writers and readers alike at conferences. She knew at an early age she wanted to write powerful heroines and fulfills that dream by writing badass empowered heroines who take charge in their paranormal worlds.

Susan grew up on a thoroughbred horse farm before moving to the big city of Dallas. She considers herself a Texan but is loyal to her home state of Arkansas. A lover of travel, she has visited several countries with many more to go on her list. She particularly loved dowsing at Stonehenge. The outdoors are a place Susan finds inspiration and can often be found in a park, at the lake, or on a road trip. She especially loves the mountains. Furry animals hold a special place in her heart, and dogs tend to seek her out as a friend.

Connect with her at susanperson.com

- facebook.com/therealsusanperson
- twitter.com/SusanM74
- instagram.com/susanm74
- amazon.com/author/susanperson
- goodreads.com/susanperson

FAE REDONE
A CLAN FAE NOVELLA - ENCHANTED ROCK IMMORTALS

Coming December 1, 2020

Death is never the end when you are Fae...

Athena survives death, but at what cost? Her connection to the elements fading; she must keep the loss a secret. Whoever heard of a Fae queen who couldn't control at least one element? Without those powers, she can't hope to save the Fae Realm and the North American Council at Enchanted Rock from the evil Kalypso.

Athena's true love, Zander, discovers a secret about his family that could change everything, maybe even the balance of power in the kingdom. Keeping the secret to himself until he can figure out the truth seems the right thing. He will risk deceiving Athena if it means he can stop Kalypso from killing her and taking over the Fae and Human Realms.

Can Zander and Athena's love endure through the secrets they keep and Kalypso's entrapment?

Fae Redone is the second Clan Fae novella in the Enchanted Rock Immortals urban fantasy romance series. If you like fast-paced worlds filled with magick and raw emotions, you'll love Susan Person's Fae or any of the Enchanted Rock Immortals novellas!

Made in the USA
Coppell, TX
06 December 2020